I0763442

Tiller

By the Author

The Education of Chauncey Doolittle

Memory's Keep

Walking Toward Home

Child to the Waters

Poems from Scorched Earth

Our Fathers' Fields

The Classical Origins of Southern Literature

A Carolina Dutch Fork Calendar

Edited by the Author

Fireside Tales. Stories of the Old Dutch Fork

Poetry and the Practical, by William Gilmore Simms

The Selected Poems of William Gilmore Simms

Selected Reviews on Literature and Civilization

Taking Root: The Nature Writings of William and Adam Summer

Tiller

James Everett Kibler, Jr.

Green Altar Books

Shotwell Publishing

Columbia, S.C.

PRODUCED IN THE REPUBLIC OF SOUTH CAROLINA BY

Green Altar Books
POST OFFICE BOX 2592
COLUMBIA, SOUTH CAROLINA 29202

A Shotwell Publication

www.ShotwellPublishing.com

Cover: "A Solitary Walk Home" by James E. Kibler. Mixed Media on Paper
Cover Design: Hazel's Dream
Interior Design: Pooja Mehra

ISBN-13: 978-0-9979393-2-3
ISBN-10: 0-9979393-2-X

10 9 8 7 6 5 4 3 2 1

To the Memory of My Grandfather,
Tira Tiller Connelly (1894-1959)

Preface

TILLER completes the four volume Clay Bank County Series begun with *Memory's Keep*. *Memory's Keep* is set in July 1975 when its main character, Trig Tinsley, is in his mid-twenties. His friend, 93 year old Pink Suber, dies on the second day of that novel. His scattered children come home to bury him. The novel began with my contemplation of the real life chair owned by the character's namesake in Upcountry South Carolina. It sat near me as I worked on various writing projects and was always in the corner of my eye. It was a cane bottomed pine chair dyed blue with indigo, and worn deeply with age. Mr. Pink's presence grew so strong that he began sitting in it, and thus the novel began.

The second work of the series, *Walking Toward Home*, is set in the year 2003 when Trig is 54 years old. Clint Blair, a major character in *Tiller*, is in veterinary school. Chauncey Doolittle, Clint's brother-in-law, appears here for the first time. He has just lost his young wife, Clint's sister, and cannot get out from under the shadow of grief. What healing comes is the result of close communal ties and immersion in nature.

The Education of Chauncey Doolittle, the third volume in the series, is set four years later in 2007. Chauncey shares the spotlight with Trig. They continue a friendship begun by their fathers many years before. Clint his just graduated and returned home. Chauncey keeps the promise to his dead wife to be Clint's guide and mentor as he continues to battle loneliness and grief.

Tiller is set in 2008-2009. Trig is 59 years old and Chauncey is 60. Chauncey's grief is lifting with a developing strong friendship with widow Dana Oxner and his wife's brother, to whom he serves as a surrogate father. In the series, community has been the primary means by which Chauncey survives the shock of loss. His journey back to normality plays to the overarching themes of regeneration and resurrection. The central plot of the series, however, is returning home. Although *Tiller* can be read alone, it is richer in the context of the other novels.

JEK, September, 2016

Tiller

One

FIFTY YEARS melted like a frosting of Southern snow in the morning sun as Trig remembered Great Grandpa Tinsley's "Young'un, happiness ain't getting what you want, but knowing how much you already got. And it ain't wanting to be somewheres else, but being thankful for where you are."

They were sitting on the porch swing that fine spring evening with the moon rising before them over the new-ploughed fields. "It's pouring water," Grandpa said of the tilted half moon slanted downward like a cup emptying. "Going to rain for sure." He'd also seen a painted box turtle crossing the road this morning, another sign you could always count on. Yesterday they'd heard the melancholy cry of the rain crows, a sign predicting wet weather within forty-eight hours. All these were powerful indicators to Grandpa. "Somehow critters know," he'd told Trig.

He had taught the grandson how to tell the number of days that rain would take in coming by counting the number of stars within the nimbus that circled the moon like a barely detectable rainbow. Those were the days you could see all the stars, before the yellow washing out of the sky by light pollution from the cities and towns.

That same evening, Grandpa had told him a story that involved Grandpa's own great grandfather, Golding Tinsley, who was a man of action to say the least and had played the part of warring ancients out of even longer memory. Grandpa told Trig that an Englishman didn't have to do much to get Grandpa Golding's Irish up and all he'd needed was blue and red body paint to fit right in with Sir William Wallace's men in their fight against the Sassenach.

The story went this way: Golding and his brother James were two of the few who'd fought for the duration of the war against Redcoats and Tories and lived to tell the tale. They'd done hard soldiering in Carolina for close to seven years and survived. Trig knew he'd not be here if Golding hadn't, for he married and sired children only after the war.

Trig kept the old Tinsley Bible in an honoured place in his living room on a walnut table Golding himself had made after the war. The Bible showed that Grandpa Golding was born in 1754. His people had come to the new land trying to escape English tyrannies in the Shamrock Isle, only to find the same old battle, and with the very same foe.

In Clay Bank District, four of the Tinsley brothers had enlisted right off. This was in July 1775 in Captain Caldwell's company of Clay Bank Rangers. In the Bible, there was preserved a yellowed and tattered scrap of paper on which Caldwell had written a line to one of the Tinsley boys: *Bring yore men up clost. Capt. C.*

Caldwell, too, was descended from the old tragic sod and knew well what they were fighting for. Under his command, the Tinsley lads did service on Sullivan's Island, north of Charles Town. This was at the Battle of Fort Moultrie in June 1776, several weeks before the famous original Fourth of July. Here they were to have been the sharp shooters to take out Peter Parker's English sailors when they came on shore, but Parker was repulsed by the guns of Moultrie behind their palmetto logs and couldn't land.

So the Tinsley boys took their rifles and came on back home to put in a late crop of corn.

Back in the Upcountry, two of Golding's brothers were killed by Tories on Fairforest Creek.

He and brother James retrieved their savagely hacked bodies and took them home. The women dressed them for burial and mourned but the men vowed revenge and wielded a sure rifle and a powerful sword. As the two brothers lay on their cooling boards, the family filed by in respect. When Golding paused there, one of the corpses' wounds opened and bled fresh blood. It was then Golding heard the voice of the ancients, as he said, calling him to a fight to the death.

Golding had a bronze-handled broad sword that had done duty against the English in an Irish Rising the century before. Grandpa said that the Tinsley who carried it in that century had survived to pass it on down to his eldest son. It was so heavy the forearm that wielded it must have been big and powerful. "He was a brave one, a tall, wirey, red-headed ornery cuss," Grandpa told Trig.

Golding and James were crack marksmen

with their long rifles, tough on a bivouac, excellent on horse back, and inexhaustible on a forced march. They were thick-chested, broad of shoulder, and strong of arm. Grandpa said Trig had inherited their build. He had their same copper-coloured hair, or more accurately, the colour of new beaten brass.

After the Battle of Stono in 1779, Golding and James escaped the calamitous surrender of Charles Town the following May. Good thing. Trig figured that imprisonment would have killed them both, almost as quick as an enemy's ball. They followed their neighbour Colonel James Williams to North Carolina. The Colonel was their grandfather on their mother's side, so besides a trusted neighbour, he was their close kinsman too. How could they not follow, if he desired to lead them?

In North Carolina, they'd learned what happened to their comrades at the Waxhaws. When these men had surrendered to the dreaded Bannie Tarleton under a flag of truce, they were cut to pieces by Bloody Ban and his men. The brothers were kin to some of the dead. When the word got to the Tinsleys and their comrades, they adopted the cry of "Tarleton's

Quarter," meaning *no quarter at all,* no mercy for their enemies. Grandpa Tinsley said that no more savage scenes could be imagined. It was as if the red clay soil was red with so many men's blood.

The Tinsley grandsons returned with Colonel Williams in August 1780 to whip the British on Enoree River at a place called Musgrove's Mill. The Tinsley boys were friends and neighbours of the heroine Mary Musgrove, who carried intelligence and hid their men from the foe under the rock ledge at Horseshoe Falls. In this battle, Williams was outnumbered two to one, but the Tinsleys and their fellow marksmen outmaneuvered the Tories and prevailed.

On the seventh of October 1780 at King's Mountain, Golding and James formed part of Grandpa Williams' advance. By this time, they called Williams "Colonel Grandpa." "We'll whoop them for you," they told him. "Colonel Grandpa," they said. "Just lead us to where you wants us to aim." And indeed Colonel Grandpa did. The Tinsleys and their fellows poured their deadly lead upon Patrick Ferguson's men. They saw Grandpa Williams die during the battle, but under Colonel Campbell, they went on to victory. They also witnessed Ferguson's bloody fall and saw compatriots mutilate his corpse. After they were through at King's Mountain, Cornwallis's left flank was no more. "Take that home across the water, you bloody Lobster Coats," they said. "You and your bloody red cross shaming the honest blue of St Andrew. As for your oath of allegiance, it's not worth two farts in a cyclone."

Grandpa Tinsley told Trig how Golding and James were then quick to attach themselves to General Thomas Sumter. "The Gamecock," as he was called, campaigned with them, slept and ate with them in their camps and led them in person like Grandpa Williams had done. He might not have been the keenest at strategies, but Sumter didn't do his generalling from some distant place like most of the other generals, and this meant a lot to the Tinsley lads.

They were with him at Fish Dam Ford on the Broad on the seventh of November 1780 and in the brave stand against Bloody Ban at Blackstock's Farm above Tyger River two weeks after that. On a hillside at Blackstock's, they once again saw their commander fall, but carried him to safety into the Old North State.

At Blackstock's, Sumter's men killed ten for every one the enemy killed of them. The signs of British defeat were piles of red coated soldiers buried in mass graves. Golding had reported that before interment could be accomplished, the old she-devil Morrigan and her crows had them quite a feast. They picked out many a bonnie blue English eye. In the little mock rivalries among the Carolina men, the Tinsleys said, "You can have your wily old frenchified Swamp Fox, we'll take our Gamecock any day over him. We fight 'em face to face with grit, spur, and steel. None of your retreat to the swamp to ambush and fight again." But then Marion was one of those subtle Huguenot sort, and was never quite fully understood by the Tinsley lads. Eye to eye and sword to sword was their way.

The Tinsleys didn't sit around waiting for wounds to heal, even General Sumter's, so they presently joined Daniel Morgan, another fiery Irishman sick of the empire's rule. They witnessed his harangue in camp the night before battle in January 1781, when the sturdy bull of a man tore his shirt from his body and stormed through his encampment exhibiting on his back the many criss-crossed scars received from an English flogging years before. "You see what the bastards did to me!" he cried as he went among his men. As the blood of passion flowed through his skin, the cross-hatched scars seemed to blaze like the campfire itself, or like meshed fiery red crosses of St Andrew. "The wounds is alive," one of them said.

Like the cry of Tarleton's Quarter, which was no quarter at all, this histrionic display kindled the brothers' souls. It was this kind of drama that best spoke to them, sharpened their edge, and made the spirited young Tinsleys the warriors they were. Others might find life simpler if you ploughed round the stump, but as for them they took it out with main force, straight ahead, no matter the sweat.

"Be-Gorrah," Golding said to James, "I'd die for such a man."

"And sure I would as well," his brother replied in his Irish lilt and with a wink of his blue eye, that had a way of flashing electric when he got excited or mad. The red colour rose in his face.

"And did you see how his scars turned to blood!" James added. "I expected them to drip like brother John's corpse wounds."

Morgan had said he'd whip Bannie Tarleton or lay down his bones, and the brothers agreed that they would too.

In Morgan, they'd found the leader who'd last. Golding said that on that cold January night of Morgan's display, he and James slept a fitful sleep. Morgan didn't sleep at all, but moved from campfire to campfire encouraging his men.

The brothers wrapped in their pinebloom coverlet and quilt that their Grandmama Williams had made, and took what shelter they could from the biting cold in a scrap of a tent. Who knew but that one or both of them would be wrapped in the same quilt as shroud come the following day. In their rough bivouac, they had with them the same cone-shaped punched tin lantern that Trig had on his mantel today, in its sacred place beneath Great Great Grandpa Tinsley's battered Confederate sword. "Fighting against odds once again," Trig had said as he hung the sword there over the lantern. "As always, fighting to be let alone, I reckon, one more time."

Trig's Grandpa continued his narration. At daybreak the Tinsley brothers formed a stalwart part of Morgan's command as they repulsed the impetuous and arrogant Green Dragoon and gave Tarleton just due. This was January 1781 at the Battle of Hannah's Cowpens. Here, they and Morgan had simply outmaneuvered and outwitted the greater numbers of their foe. The battle was swift and quickly decided. Though it felt like ages, the fighting took less than twenty minutes. No fewer minutes had decided so much in the history of the land.

Grandpa Tinsley said that yes, truly now, in Morgan they knew they'd found their man. Golding declared he'd walk through hell itself to follow him. And Morgan singled them out for his attentions, knowing the skilled horsemen and fierce fighters they were. So the brothers stayed with him and united with Nathaniel Greene, then made the celebrated trek to Virginia, and on back to Guilford Court House and its well-fought field. Golding had not yet turned twenty-six. Brother James was not quite twenty-three.

Golding told that in March '81, after chasing Cornwallis to Deep River and Ramsay's Mill, they came with the main army back to Camden's Hobkirk's Hill. They were with Greene at Ninety

Six that May, and what they did there caused the British to evacuate that outpost and retreat closer to their getaway ships at Charles Town.

Five months later, saw them a part of the loyal band at Yorktown. Grandpa Tinsley surmised, "You may be sure they didn't stand idle there, with arms and glory at their feet." Golding said they even got a glimpse of Cornwallis himself and witnessed the white sails of the French ships that had boxed the English in. No fleeing to London for them.

Even after the Yorktown surrender, and back home on their father's soil, the two boys mustered in as part of Colonel Hayes' command in November '81. The Tories in Upcountry South Carolina had not surrendered at Yorktown, and the animosities of neighbour against neighbour still raged. The fight was now more grudge than war, more the pay back of blood feud than politics or ideals. There were still many old wrongs to set right. As folks knew, it didn't take a very big person to carry a grudge anyway. And Golding and James, truth to tell, just loved a good fight. They had it soon enough. The Tory Bloody Bill Cunningham had surprised their commander Hayes in skirmish that November

'81. Hayes had been with Colonel Williams and the Tinsleys at King's Mountain and before, such that Grandpa Williams had counted him, as he said, as a man of his own family. The Tinsleys felt the same.

Hayes had stationed at Little River at Mr. Edgehill's, east of Little River, on the old Charles Town Road, between new plantations called Belfast and Antrim. Belfast house, built not too long after peace came, is still to be seen. It was the family seat of the Simpsons, who, like the Tinsleys, had come from the same mother sod.

Edgehill's dwelling was built of logs and by the distress of the day, had to do double duty as fort. Hayes was there with his men. Golding remembered how Hayes had stood at his blacksmith's forge making horseshoes. Bloody Bill surprised the command, and the men were driven inside the cabin. Gunfire ensued and men were killed.

A ramrod tipped with flax and saturated with tar was shot flaming onto the cedar shake roof. Golding said that quicker than an eye-blink, the house was ablaze. Hayes and his party, on a promise of good quarter, surrendered straight way. But Cunningham had learned much about war from the Green Dragoon.

He selected Hayes and young Daniel Williams to be hanged. Daniel was a son of Colonel Grandpa Williams, who'd fallen at the British defeat at King's Mountain at the head of the Tinsleys' command. Cunningham selected him for payback. Golding and James were little Dan's nephews and good friends.

The Tinsley boys witnessed the whole thing. Cunningham was in the process of hanging Hayes and Williams from a pole of a fodder-stack, when Daniel's younger brother Joseph stepped forward. He was a lad of sixteen, and another of Colonel Williams' sons. Joseph had known Cunningham from the time he was a little child. They were born on neighbouring lands.

Golding recalled that with the blazing cabin behind them, he heard the lad say, "Captain Cunningham, how shall I go home and tell Mama you've hanged brother Daniel?"

Cunningham replied that he'd save him the trouble and had his men seize and hang him up by his brother and Hayes. In the process, the added weight caused the fodder pole to fall. The three men had their hands behind their backs and couldn't defend themselves, so Cunningham and his men hewed them to pieces with their swords.

Then the work of death commenced in earnest on both sides. Each man of the two companies had the right to kill or spare as he pleased. Golding and James, along with friends Dunlap and Cummins, were four of Hayes' men who scrapped to survive.

As Grandpa Tinsley related, this was the last of the bloody trials of the Revolution for them. The British power was boxed up in Charles Town, that is, until December '82, when their tall ships set sail.

James said to Golding then, "Now an American Irishman can breathe free for a time and walk on free land without being pestered by the Sassenach." He reckoned that now maybe no more of their Presbyterian meeting houses would be burned down as sedition shops, as the English had labeled them. To this, Golding gave three huzzas for the green Shamrock Isle and the new land where they could be rid once and for all of English rule.

Golding Tinsley lived many years after the war. The old Bible recorded he died peacefully on his farm on 11 May 1851, having reached the great age of ninety-six years. His son Isaac survived him to bear four stalwart sons.

The old warrior was interred with the honours of war. Not less than two thousand comprised his funeral cortege as they laid him to rest there in the countryside near the old Tinsley home. His grandsons buried his battered old broadsword with him. They put it at the ready in his right hand on his chest as he'd directed them, "In case there's any bloody damn English around on the waking up day."

Two

TRIGGERFOOT KNEW the story like it happened yesterday, that and many more besides. He never tired of telling the tale of how Great-Great-Grandpa Golding got him a wife after the war.

"If it would've been this easy with Becky Sue Glenn," he told Chauncey, "Today, I'd have me a hundred grandchildren riding horsey on my knee."

Triggerfoot's story would usually run this way:

"War over and Golding was scratching out a living by himself on part of his daddy's land there on Little River. He was about to turn thirty. His younger brother James was married nearby and already had two little cotton-top young'uns running about his farmhouse door. They'd come back to normal as best they could and had adopted the wisdom of not interfering with something that aint bothering you none. Living and letting live was their way.

"Golding was tired of the bachelor life and of doing his own field and house work too. For seven years in his twenties, he'd always lived in camp with men, when most men were marrying and settling down, so his social graces, though not lacking, weren't, you might say, ample neither.

"He was still a mite shy around women, who he rightly deemed a great mystery. He'd learned very quick that you'd better know what you were doing or else leave them alone. Compared to them, war wasn't so complicated after all.

"One Saturday morning while he was straightening up his house, Golding said to himself, 'I must have me a wife. I'm tired of sleeping by myself, I'm bout to starve for good food, and this place looks like hell.' So he began to scrub and primp, as best he could, but didn't have much success.

"Golding was wary about the venture, but still he vowed he'd not come through seven hard years of war to be scared of a girl. So he put on his best walnut brown linsey-woolsey coat that fit his sturdy frame and went to the stable for Ball.

"Ball was a high-stepping coal-black stallion

off of which Golding had shot and killed a British officer during the war. He'd captured horse, bridle, fine silver-studded saddle, and all.

"Mounting Ball a little after noon, he rode up the wagon road a couple of miles to the house of James Kelly, he whose sons had fought beside the Tinsley boys a time or two during the war. The father himself had shouldered a long rifle at times. They'd fight, then they'd go home to farm. In camp, the sons were always talking about their six sweet pretty sisters and he'd even once had a glimpse of one when she'd brought some homespun shirts and a quilt to her brothers.

"Golding got to the Kelly farmstead about one, and hailing Kelly, who was walking his fields, Kelly invited him to 'light and sit awhile.' 'Good to see you, Mr Tinsley,' Kelly said. 'I walks my fields every day. A planter's steps is like manure to his land.'

"But Golding kept his saddle and told Kelly his mind—that he'd come to see if he could get one of his six girls for a wife.

"'Well, Golding, you'll just have to go in and see the girls about that. They's pretty touchy and strong minded about such things.'

"So Golding rode up to the house, got down, hitched Ball to the gatepost, and went in. Kelly had caught up to him and accompanied him in.

"They found two of the girls carding cotton, one spinning, one cooking at the hearth, one mending, and one sewing a shirt for their pa.

"Their pa said, 'Girls, Tinsley here has come to get one of you for a wife.' Then turning to Golding, 'Well, Tinsley, which one will you have?'

"'I'll take Agnes,' Golding said. It was she he'd glimpsed in camp several years before. He hadn't forgotten her, and she was even more beautiful today. Her flaxen curls fell in shiny soft ringlets about her face. A little colour came to her forehead and cheeks.

"Kelly then asked, 'Agnes, will you have him?' and without a pause, she answered, 'Yes, Pa, I believe I will.'

"So about two o'clock, Agnes got up behind Golding on Ball, as couples often rode double on horseback in them days, sort of like a pair on a motorcycle today. She'd gathered a few of her things in a big split oak basket, and Golding put them in his saddle bags. He tried not to notice the delicate things some of them were.

"They rode to preacher Rogers, where they were married before suppertime.

"They went on back to Golding's for the night, then next morning rode over to Kelly's, where Golding ate him a big hearty breakfast prepared by his new mother-in-law and the girls. The brothers wanted to rib him a little about his fierce appetite, but minded their manners for the most part. They were glad to have Tinsley in the family. War had shown them what he was made of. Nothing tells you more about a man than working at a hard job or fighting shoulder to shoulder with him.

"It was a happy match, faithful to death, and fruitful too. There were six young'uns in as many years. 'Making up for lost time,' Golding said. In one year, Agnes throwed deuce, as Golding put it, the twins, Tira Tiller and Ira Hunter. Golding, who'd chosen all his boys' names, figured hunting and tilling were their traditions on the land, and as honourable as any the world had known. General Washington, whom he always spoke of with reverence, had been good at both. And if it was good enough for General Washington, it was good enough for him and his."

"Good enough for me too," Trig would usually add at the end of the tale.

He descended from Tira Tiller and was still tilling the soil.

As for good judgement in such things as these, he'd usually conclude, "Good judgement comes from experience, and a lot of that comes from bad judgement. If you've got proper good sense, and the gumption to go with it, you can make your way."

Three

WHEN TRIG would tell his friends the story of Golding's quick, on-the-spur marriage and how successful it was, either Kildee or Chauncey or some other listener at the store would invariably ask, "Without a careful courtship how did the pair know they'd get along? How could such a marriage last? What if the couple found they just didn't have anything in common to build a relationship on? Better a long engagement or even living together for a space to judge compatibility, don't you think?" Another might add, "And then some women swear there has to be a forty thousand dollar wedding to make it last. But even that don't always work. Sometimes the couple don't get the wedding bill paid off before the divorce."

Chauncey had about decided he now finally had the answer to this question, as mystifying at first as the question seemed.

He'd come to understand that the answer was really quite simple, and it lay in the phrase "just nothing in common to build upon." On the contrary, there was no questioning that Golding and his new wife had everything in common to build on. He started enumerating what. They'd both come from farms, and from the same neighbourhood. Their families would live around them and there'd be no modern squabble of a pair from different places, maybe even regions, deciding who would sacrifice and go to the other's home. Perhaps go to neither's as a compromise, and both then lose family. Telephoning and jetting for visits just wasn't the same.

Stability. That was the key word. Not so many fracturings and tearings of the social fabric of home. Not so much difference to have to come to grips with and settle between.

Chauncey felt their world was a lot like a quilt, sewed communally from cloth gathered from family, neighbours, and friends. Its pieces were fitted together in careful and intricate design, then stitched over in rows like furroughs to give the cloth extra strength. The result was harmony and beauty so quiet and natural you'd almost not see. It made cold nights comfortable and warm.

Sustainability was the new buzz word for those in the know. His take was that the stable life of old did the sustaining of people. It wasn't just that you lived in such a way as not to use up resources. Human resources, if seen in the right way, were as important as natural resources, it seemed to him. Sustainability meant continuity. It was the opposite of fragmentation, alienation, isolation, and rootlessness, those hallmarks of the unsustainable, so-called progressive modern way.

Chauncey knew that to conserve meant that you had to conserve both natural and human resources at one and the same time.

He figured that in the old days the couple probably would have gone to the same church or at least one nearby. There'd not be that major decision of whose they'd attend, not to mention if they'd attend at all. Not to mention what god they'd worship. There wasn't but one.

Their values in all things that mattered were in accord.

They ate the same food, sang the same songs, dressed the same way, danced the same dances, played the same games. The husband went to the fields much like her father and grandfather before. The wife did the same duties at home, raised the children with the same values of old. They read the same Scripture their kin always had, memorised the same stately lines of the King James. Its poetry dispensed the same wisdom, tested through centuries. They enjoyed the same enjoyments, regretted the same losses, mourned in the same way the deaths of their kin, and laid them to rest in communal soil.

They all liked porches and working together—quiltings, molasses boilings, corn pullings and shuckings, peanut pickings, and hog butchering days when it got cold enough for the meat to save. Then there were the fall hunts and the summer barbecues, the church reunions and revivals. They did everything as family—bonded in time and ritual, knowledge bred in the bone. When they married, families instead of individuals wed. With them, in everyday life there was more ritual than routine, a way both Trig and Chauncey were trying to continue to observe.

Chauncey could vouch that in the spring they must have waked to the same whippoorwill calls, for so did he. Together, they heard the bob-white's calls in the summer fields, the racket the wild turkeys made each spring morning in the woods at mating time. The same blue-birds must have followed the plough, carrying the newly warming sky on their back. They both must have shared the same love of the land. They saw the same sunsets behind hills, fields, and trees. "I'd be throwed away in any other place," they'd most likely say. No flat landscape for them. It would be as foreign as Timbuctoo.

So much in common then, these things and hundreds more, shared assumptions and attachments, a continuous harmony. They'd sewn up fragments and pieces of colour to bring things together in a comfortable, sturdy quilt of harmonious design. The stitches were put in painstakingly and with strong thread, and held.

Chauncey knew from his marriage to Hoyalene that it worked this way. He'd seen this in his own life. It was from his and his mama's and daddy's own experience and those of his neighbours and kin, both close and distant too, both present and past, that he'd drawn his conclusion today.

This anchoring firmly in place and knowing your neighbours from childhood on—that and church-going made the pool from which couples came. "That's how they met in the first place!" it finally dawned on him.

"No wonder the divorce rate has soared," Kildee said just the other day. "People come together with nothing in common. Following a job wherever it leads. Thinking convenience, money, and sex will be the cure-alls."

"Maybe even good to marry somebody in your own family," he'd added only half-jokingly, because most everybody in Clay Bank County were related in more than one way.

"We're all cousins here," Lula Bess had declared. "And that's sure a common foundation to build on."

"And why you always have to think twice or maybe three times before you say anything bad about anyone. You'd be talking about somebody's kin," Kildee chimed in. "It makes for good manners. You're extra careful what you say. Daddy always told us that the person with the best command of the language is the one who can hold his tongue about such things."

Some newcomers gathered this wisdom more quickly than others, or at least those among them who fitted in and stayed.

Their world for all its casualness, was more

deliberate than it first seemed. People were more careful, less rash, in how they dealt with the scene. Great boxes in warehouses often read

FRAGILE. HANDLE WITH CARE.

Chauncey figured that this would have been a better caution for handling women and men. Like a dropped crystal vase, you can't unsay a cruel or angry word. It was much more than good manners after all. His father always said that meanness don't just happen overnight and folks who don't have good manners are probably missing more than just manners. The older Chauncey got, the more accurate the observations seemed.

He'd learned that in most of the states, it was illegal to marry a first cousin. When he'd mentioned this at Kildee's Store, old Farmer Lyman, who was eighty-four years old, had said: "If cousins hadn't been able to marry in the old days, nobody'd got married. Today, there'd be nobody here."

Chauncey was proud of his place, proud that his state had made no laws to keep cousins from marrying. Just like it was the last state to make divorce easily legal too.

"Probably just two other ways the world thinks we're backward," Clint had said. "But who the heck cares."

Clint shared Chauncey's attitude. "Some of the people I met at college laughed and said that in the South our family trees don't branch. But at least we still got trees and not a pre-fab virtual world made out of concrete and steel and with nothing alive that has living roots at all. They don't like us because we're not progressive and like traditional things. That makes it harder to make money off of us. And for these kind of folks, that's what people's for. Sure thing, it's not for young'uns. Most of them, they abort, and they make certain the law allows it to be easy. Young'uns are inconvenient and cost too much."

Not long ago, Chauncey had occasion to give Clint a little history lesson. First government to stage a divorce revolution was the French Jacobins, he'd said. Then the foreign rule in South Carolina after the war ended in 1865 forced the same measures on the helpless state. The radicals revoked the strictest divorce law in the U. S. and made it the most liberal. When the outsiders were run off in 1876, one of the first things the restored government did was to revive the state's strict divorce law.

Chauncey had concluded that family constructs the lower basic orders of society, which in turn construct the state, and that no legitimate state will strip the province, village, and family of their traditional prerogatives. What strengthens the stability of the family makes a healthy state possible. Clint understood well and had not taken his marriage to Ida lightly. The couple had talked about this too. Marriage was a holy estate and a sacrament.

Yes, Chauncey and Clint knew their history, not so much from history classes at college but from family experience. Their place and their people had come through much, fire and sword, wars' pillage, laws imposed on them, and an official disdain of what they held dear. So what else was new? When Chauncey was born in 1949, the state was still paying off Reconstruction debts for money pocketed by the outsiders. Chauncey had learned that story well. It wasn't the Depression alone that had impoverished the land. He took it personally. It wasn't a distant abstract to be debated. He lived its truth. There had been many times that he and the people around him had gone without.

And now his people were singled out for scorn and as a model of what not to be and do. Clint always said, "Fine, if the new ways worked. It may not be the things we do, but the things we don't do, that we'll be remembered for." He and Chauncey agreed that now the alien's hateful ways were shown to be bankrupt and a dead end, exposed for the hollowness at their core. The new world was erected on shifting sands that nothing genuine or lasting could be built upon.

The two friends talked about that a lot. Nothing sustainable there, either of resources or men. Chauncey remarked that their material idols were being revealed to have feet of clay. Their ways could lead only to strife, destruction, and frustration. The aim of their planning was commodification. Everything became commodity, and finally even women and men. People became disposable and as easy to throw away as a candy wrapper.

The lowliest folks around here could have warned them of that. In fact, some of them had tried, but arrogance always turns a deaf ear and prepares its own doom, especially when that doom approaches so near. The enemy had been playing a dangerous game, gambling with what makes humans human as the stakes. Chauncey could have told them that. So could most of his Clay Bank County friends. It was more than just a pair of tall buildings tumbling down. Chauncey saw the symbolism of the whirlwind of business forms in triplicate, ticker tape, stock sheets, business accounts—scattered like confetti onto the waters of the New Jersey shore as far as two miles away. To him it was the fatal fallout of hollow values with plenty of wrong to go around. Dead ends could only yield death. Tragically, it was the logical outcome.

He recalled the eight words in four unpunctuated lines of Eliot's great poem

Falling towers
Jerusalem Athens Alexandria
Vienna London
Unreal

The old shared long-built beliefs, dearly and so slowly won, that shored us were now become shattered and unreal in a wasted land with no ties to the transcendent, and with only matter and money in a world flatly, empirically perceived.

"You can't keep on converting nature and the spirit into money and expect to live," Chauncey had said to Clint. About the progressive world's scorn of them, Chauncey and the people around him echoed Clint's "Who cares." It wasn't a question. It was more an emphatic statement of fact, and edged with the attitude, "Go to hell." For some time, Clint had been seeing bumper stickers in the country that read in bold letters

WE DON'T CARE HOW YOU DID IT UP NORTH.

Clint had a new saying he'd learned from his oldest brother Joe-Pratt. Joe-Pratt was tired of the marketing hype he saw every day in ads. "New and Improved!" they'd declare. Joe-Pratt said: "New and improved can't beat tried and true." Knowing this truth protected them against all sorts of folly and placed them safely outside the commodifying society that was run by hucksters on the make and on the take, opportunists who discarded planned obsolescent things, and finally even threw people and places away. They would pick up and move on a whim without giving it a thought. They would exchange spouses capriciously. There was nothing continuous or stable in their lives with the exception of acquiring material things.

Chauncey reckoned that the same blood, distant or cousins, gave common bond and common cause and made for cohesiveness in the most human way, no matter how little else the couple shared. Careful courtships, long engagements, even trial living together, whatever the new way, the most current statistics showed that one out of two of these new marriages failed. And that's not good odds for success and certainly no commendation for the progressive modern way. Chauncey felt *unhealthy* to be the operative word to describe the modern scene.

In the case of Golding Tinsley and Agnes Kelly, the husband, his father-in-law, and his new brothers-in-law had all fought the British side by side, shared the same camp fires, ate the same meagre rations, marched the same marches, lost the same friends, shared the same set-backs and victories. They had the same Irish blood and saw the world in similar way. It was natural for each to seek out that which was familiar and comforting, not confrontational, divisive, like water and oil.

Chauncey had come to thinking now that he might entertain the idea of marrying again. But for now, he'd not puzzle his brain. He'd just sit on Kildee's porch with him and Lula Bess, and rock. "Experiencing new cultures," that facile goal of the rootless globalist, was not for him. Chauncey would mutter, "Such a glib, mindless phrase that was! Experiencing new cultures indeed, when you hadn't even established one of your own. No not for me." The concept of a world without borders was absurd to him.

So was anything that screamed it was new and improved. He had struggled and honourably sought to know his own, what was genuine and had lasted, and was still learning new things every day. On some days the revelations even startled and surprised. They often included things about himself and those closest him. The more he learned, the more he knew he lacked. That was what he now called "knowing yourself."

"How few folks nowadays ever know who they are," he said to Kildee and Bess.

"They don't take the time to stop and ask,"

Kildee replied. "Don't have a place to start from either. First, you got to be from somewhere. Too much moving around."

"Cousin Dana says that's the way it is up in Charlotte," added Lula Bess. "She calls it the geography of nowhere. Everything's based on money, getting and spending, and mindless routine and a virtual life."

"It's not just Charlotte. It's gotten that way a lot of places now," Kildee said. "Pa always told us that some place is better than anywhere." He added, "It can't be bought by an airline ticket or berth on a cruise ship."

After a pause, Chauncey said, "Well, Dana ought to come home."

"That's what we tell her all the time." Lula Bess got up and called it a night.

"We're working on it," she said. "I think we've about got her convinced."

When she'd gone, Kildee remarked, "It's damn hard to get along with someone in a marriage if you can't get along with yourself, and to get along with yourself you first got to know who you are." To him and Lula Bess, it was as simple as that.

Chauncey knew that while that kind of stability

was common enough around Clay Bank, it was rare out there in the push and shove world of concrete and steel, a place where only boxes of commodities got marked **FRAGILE. HANDLE WITH CARE**. A bitter irony, this, but so telling of the nature of the thing. It was the value system that showed the priorities of the winners of this contest over what matters in the world, of those who had defined *success* for the world. He figured that his and Kildee's and Trig's side had lost big-time in this great tug of war, but he knew that the winner's world was eaten out empty. It had a rot at what passed for its core, a weakness, a void, and an essential lack that would bring its cold and sterile virtual cathedrals of commerce tumbling down. Their collapse would crush all beneath them and leave only a fall-out of ticker-tape, sales records, and pink, blue, and yellow papers in triplicate to litter the shores of the desolate land. Success, as his own father and grandfather before him had defined it, was not the *how much* but the *how* of achievement. That little shared assumption of a value system had never been far from Chauncey's mind, and he'd reinforced it in Clint. Leastways, there were indications to make him think he had.

Kildee and Chauncey talked on awhile before Chauncey pointed Blue Bessie toward home. He drove with his windows down. Somewhere in the distance he could hear a whippoorwill and still further off hound voices on a hunt. The summer night was a clear one, and he had the welcome company of stars. "Real," he found himself saying aloud to the fine pin-pricks of light through which heaven leaked down onto a parched, dark world.

Four

CHAUNCEY REFLECTED back to when he'd taken Trig to see Hardy Rogers, his dentist friend in Spartanburg. Although it was nearly two years ago, he remembered the particularities of that day as if it were yesterday. The deed done, Trig's hurting wisdom tooth pulled, and with bloody mouth and all, Trig wouldn't be dissuaded. "You sure you don't want to get on home and get to bed?" he'd asked his friend. But they were only a few blocks away, and Trig didn't get to town all that often. So Chauncey humoured him because doing so was harmless and there was reason to his rhyme.

Trig's request was simple enough. He wanted Chauncey to drive him downtown to Morgan Square to see once again the bronze statue of the great man. His folks had always remembered Daniel Morgan like family. Through so many stories passed down, he was like a neighbour who still lived just down the lane. Trig had never read a history book about him. He didn't have to. The tales his grandpa told him when he was a boy of seven, eight, and nine, had remained burned in his brain. A history teacher in high school had added dates and places as the skeleton the real flesh hung upon.

So Chauncey had situated his friend in the passenger seat complete with spit cup for his pulled tooth and off they drove. Trig didn't say much, only a grunt for yes and no. His mouth was still numb and the packing further prevented any impulse. Not being able to talk was a torture as bad as the day's ordeal; but on this day of trial, he cared less about that than he usually would. It was probably the nitrous oxide and the shots Rogers had put in his gum. There was something to be said for kicking back and just taking it all in.

Chauncey resisted the fleeting impulse to play the truck radio. He fiddled with the dial a few seconds but finally clicked it off.

Trig looked over at his friend and managed a thanks.

"No problem," Chauncey returned.

From Pine Street, they turned left onto West Main. Beside them was a multi-story office tower and a sterile looking plaza that needed trees. The store fronts of old buildings were at best shabby genteel, but even in their look of disrepair, Chauncey thought how good it was they'd escaped the rage of being progressively plasticised and covered over with aluminum after World War II.

For this prime time of a work day, there was little traffic. Few people were to be seen outside. No doubt the shoppers were at the various climate controlled malls on the periphery of the city, or off to shop in Greenville or Charlotte where they could really feel in style.

He and Trig kept silence as the facades flowed smoothly by.

Then there was the great bronze man on his tall column with his back to the river once again, or so it seemed to Trig. He knew from family stories going back to Golding himself, who was there, how General Morgan had placed his men facing the enemy with the river behind them so he'd make extra sure that even if they had the inclination, they wouldn't run. Trig had always laughed at this, but Grandpa had assured him that Golding and James didn't need that persuasion to fight an Englishman. They hadn't signed up the year before the war really began and stuck at it a month after it was over to need a river to persuade them of anything.

Neither did the gleaming man who looked down from his heavy column there, his wide, strong shoulders arched to the world.

Yes, Trig knew that when it came to what they called the spawn of Oliver Cromwell, Golding and James were always itching for a scrap. And they shared that with the Irish, Welsh, and Scots-Irish of their neighbourhood. From what Golding had passed down to them, Morgan must have liked such a scrap as much as they did, or more.

The city had recently given the statue a good cleaning and turned it to face north, north toward Hannah's Cow Pens, as it had originally stood before some progressive city planner had reoriented it for convenience and utility. Now the autumn sunlight burnished the bronze and gave it a rich glow. The colour was in perfect harmony with the season. It reminded Chauncey of a stubble field, stacks of fodder, and bales of new cut hay. He was proud of the city for not forgetting its past in keeping up this remembrance. So often with growth, money, and progress, this was not the case. It was certainly not the Chamber of Commerce's usual way. Trig called the group the Chamberpot when he had occasion to mention it at all.

"They're sure not the sharpest tool in the shed," he'd say. "They aim for the quick buck fix and never see the long-term disaster. It's like they done stepped off the curb one time too many." He thought a moment as Chauncey described how the so-called progressives of the world were always in the news, pushing this economic strategy or that—new plants, a new lake for tourism, impounding his free-flowing Tyger. Talking. Talking. Talking. Scheming. Scheming.

After a pause, Trig replied, "You know, Chaunts, men are like barrels. The emptiest ones make the most noise."

So General Morgan stood in his fringed buckskin, the feather plume in his hat, his sword's empty scabbard steadying his stance, his sharp-pointed sword drawn.

Chauncey circled the monument and Trig's gaze rotated with the movement. He never lost sight of the bronze face. Looking up, with Morgan against the bright sky, Trig felt that the old wagoner fixed his gaze upon him. It wasn't north towards Cowpens that he looked. It was towards him.

"You're watching me, ain't you?" Trig mumbled to himself. Chauncey couldn't make out exactly what his friend said, but from the look on his face it was serious.

Then Morgan was behind them. Trig looked at the side view mirror and saw him disappear, first feet, then knees, torso, and finally the plume.

"Thanks," Trig managed to say through the packing. This time Chauncey didn't reply, but after a pause, tuned in the local country station, where Keith Urban was singing a tune.

"If that ain't some name for a country star," he said to Trig. "Tells a lot about the state country music's in. It's more about tight jeans and tattoos nowadays. Not much about song. Guess like everything Southern, when it gets popular because it's genuine, the money-men from way off take over and they spoil it all by making it fake. And why? Because they don't have a clue. Same with NASCAR. When they took the race from Darlington, where it all started in the first place, I was through with them."

Trig wanted to say, "But they usually know

how to make money. That's their specialty. That is, till they kill the goose that lays the eggs." He didn't speak, however, for still in his mind was Morgan's fringed left arm parallel with the earth atop an empty scabbard, empty for action, the sword being in his strong right hand drawn and at the ready, his body twisting muscular to the fray.

Keith Urban indeed. The bronze man on the column was about as far from Urban as you could get.

The strains of the country song sounded like white noise to Trig. He was glad when Chauncey decided he'd had enough.

Before leaving the city, there was one more place Trig persuaded his friend to go. And now they were there. The heavy iron gates of Magnolia Cemetery clanged behind them and Trig stood, his hat in his hand. **WILLIAM WALKER, A.S.H. 1809-1875** the granite read. Chauncey knew the story too. Walker, Old Singin' Billy of the last century, had been author and compiler of the *Southern Harmony*, a book of shape-note hymns by which the congregations of old learned their tunes. Since he'd published it in 1835, he'd walked and ridden thousands of miles carrying his book to set up his singing schools. Into the fastnesses of the mountains, he went, crossing the French Broad and writing one of his most powerful tunes:

Far o'er the hills the mountains rise
Their summits tow'r toward the skies
But far above them I must dwell
Or sink beneath the flames of hell....

Walker's note in the hymn book said he'd learned the tune for the song at his dear mother's knee. She was Susan Jackson from Ireland and the tune had crossed the waves from Erin to their own green land there on Fairforest Creek. The ship was tossed, but its tiller had guided her true and now the Atlantic waves had got caught up in the rhythm of song.

Trig was known for his voice and skill at fiddle and banjo. Singin' Billy was one of his favourites to sing and always got requests whenever he sang.

Chauncey remembered the story that before he died, Singin' Billy had said he'd rather have the initials **A. S. H.**, Author of *Southern Harmony*, after his name than **PRES.** And so his dutiful children had done what he'd desired. Walker was justly proud of what he'd accomplished. In Richmond in 1862, he'd had time to become friends with Stonewall Jackson. They'd come together as kin, Walker's mama being a Jackson relative. They also had in common the love of hymns, and who better than Billy for General Jackson to lean on there.

Both fought for the farm way of life against the Cromwells of their time. They saw the conflict as another case of Puritans beating up on their people, the same Puritan breed that had invaded the lands of their Irish and Welsh forebears. The **PRES.** at the time Billy had said it, was now a politician, not a statesman like Washington or Jefferson, both farmers also, two of their own, back in a time when the Republic was real and not just a name. Now Billy felt the **PRES.** would do anything for the job, cheat, steal, or lie. Those two earlier farmers didn't want the job, and had to be persuaded, coerced, and cajoled into taking it, doing so not for power or perks, but out of duty. This recent election had really shown him how severely limited the political pool was. Chauncey couldn't care a fig who won and registered his disdain by not voting at all. For him, opting out was his vote of no confidence in the political scene, and so it was with many of his neighbours and friends.

Times had truly changed. The city in which Morgan and Walker were memorialised had lost its economy to China, and had played to German automobiles to keep it afloat. To Chauncey, "Beware of entangling alliances," seemed to echo among the ragged line of tombstones.

The two friends had stood there silent for a good while. Then Trig needed the spit cup he'd left in the truck and wouldn't spit on the cemetery ground.

In the truck once again, Chauncey had asked his friend, "Anywhere else you feel you just got to go?"

"Nope," Trig replied, and this time they'd headed for home.

"Old Doc Watson," Chauncey said after awhile. "He's still carrying on. He says that Singin' Billy is the most important influence on his song. I sure like his 'Down to the River to Pray.' It has all the feel of Singin' Billy through and through. 'Angel Band' comes straight out of the *Harmony.* Wonder if Keith Urban could manage such a song?"

Chauncey knew Urban was a gentle enough, well-intentioned young man. He and Nicole. He was Kidman's most recent groom. They'd had to separate so short after their marriage for him to check into a rehab clinic for some kind of abuse. Chauncey was vague on the details.

Urban may have had talent once, but was too glittery, too soft, like a sponge, too bland and fast food processed, like potted meat or processed cheese, too easily moulded by Hollywood, and now closely connected with that material world of false show. Man become commodity. Talent packaged and commodified. Flesh poured into the shape of jeans like meat in the can. About their world, the world of William Walker and Daniel Morgan, the new musicians wouldn't have a clue, or at least Chauncey didn't think so.

But Trig hadn't answered Chauncey's question about Urban. His mind was preoccupied by shuffling back and forth from the bronze man on his column to Singin' Billy's stone.

Sweet fields arrayed in living green. And rivers of delight, he'd hummed Singin' Billy's words in an interior song, took a spit in his cup, and closed his eyes as the truck drove on.

Chauncey recalled how nearing home he'd

given his usual index finger wave above the steering wheel to the driver of a passing truck, and the driver had returned it. He remembered how he could once again drive with one hand instead of gripping the wheel till his knuckles turned white, how the curves and turns were so familiar he felt he could maneuver the route with his eyes closed. That was a memorable day with Trig. Morgan and Walker had given direction to their utilitarian day. As usual, Trig was the tiller steering true.

Here at home today, Chauncey was trying to get his feelings down in verse. In his reading alcove with a view of his fields before him, he translated emotions into lines. As the ink flowed in their regular way, the rhythm reminded him of ploughing. *Verse*, the Latin word—a turn at the end of the ploughed row. Back to origins. Keep it in the row and plough the row straight. Although he understood free verse form and what occasioned it, he liked the traditional line. A finished poem should look like a field ploughed in good order, in good tilth, as his father would put it. A poem out of kilter looked like a slovenly man's attempts at putting in crops, rows that the weeds and grass had taken over and nearly erased. Or better, the jagged disconnects and fracturings of the contemporary scene.

His feelings today might best be sung. *Sweet fields arrayed in living green. And rivers of delight,* he hummed. He wished he'd written lines as memorable as these, and set to music too. He recalled a good Southern poet's saying that one fine song is worth all the graver volumes of history. Singin' Billy had been responsible for that *one fine song* in both "Amazing Grace" and "French Broad." Of the two, Chauncey preferred the latter, although the great world did not agree. They had made "Amazing Grace" into a secular anthem of feel-good humanism, especially after the addition of that "ten thousand years" stanza, written by Harriet Beecher Stowe. Chauncey reflected on how Singin' Billy would have hated what had become of his song and to what purposes it had been used.

There in the quiet, he was now working out words he'd been drumming in his head all morning as he'd gone about the rhythm of his chores. He understood quite well how the work songs of Ireland and Scotland got made. Certain repeated motions of the body in their hard performance got made easier by the rhythm of words. Communal work. How much better than the solitary performance or the assembly line. The day's work accompanied, driven, transformed, mated, and celebrated in song. He thought how his own private definition of a poem might be a good and accurate one after all: a celebration of your oneness with the world. The narcissistic flaying of the soul in miserable isolation was not for him, was not his way. He hoped his poems to be communal acts, like the old Greek and Latin odes, tying him to people, places, and things, and for all times.

He put himself back in the row and the words came. They had an appropriateness on the page and weren't bounded by it. That was what he was after. Invisible ink. It was the rhythm mated to right words that had worked themselves into his marrow more than half way before he sat down there at his window. And behind it all was Singin' Billy, his fellow son of Tyger. He felt close to him now. Billy had seen the same green landscape of hills, the same stream. The rhythm of this place had gotten into both their souls and the fountain of creation had issued from the same deep bedrock in the clear refreshing waters that could only quench his thirst.

Chauncey had been holding a single shiny white bean as he sat thinking. He was going to plant it when the proper time came next spring. He had already prepared the plot, digging the soil deep and manuring and composting with the dark rich smelling mould. The soil would lie fallow during winter soaking up the clean fresh air. The bean was an heirloom passed down for who knows how many generations in his and the Epting families. All he knew other than that, is that those who ate the cooked meal from it had, like Trig and Grandpa Tinsley, called the bean "jawlicious" for its quality of "Lord, pass me some moreness." His pen poured out a tribute of ploughed lines,

A seed is memory,
Mutely following pattern
Destined to fulfill, return.
It can be counted on
To be itself and no other,
To spring no surprises.
Quietly content in the universe contained
Within hard bounds,
A seed is patience concentrated down—
Epitome of waiting, essence of itself,
A truth to trust,
Tradition's firmest friend.

Chauncey read his new lines through and was well enough satisfied for now. No doubt months later he'd make adjustments here and there after the poem had cooled.

He always felt better after writing. Somehow the world clarified a little and he felt more complete. His brain rounded out and was not left hanging. The creative act, for him, how important to wellness.

He sat thinking all men are given a spark at birth, a little bit of the Creator's fire. Then the person either used it properly or twisted it to other ends. Fire could be helpful or could destroy. Writers, painters, sculptors, builders, all those who worked creatively and honourably with their minds and hands in making, were usually the folks he'd trust. Those who turned their creative fire to greed did most of the damage to the world. It was they who commodified the earth, clear-cut the forests he loved in order to plump their bank accounts, paved the fertile soil, made wars and scorched the land, those who needed power trips to validate empty lives that had nothing to give and could only take, those who turned the life force of man and nature into cash and had a cash-register evaluation of all things, those who abused people and the land. They were the rapers and plunderers of the world, the barterers and hucksters operating through deceit and scam. It was so ironic to Chauncey that these gatherers and spenders who lay waste to the spirit were the unhappiest of men. Unfulfilled. Needing more commodities to fill a lack that couldn't be filled with the things they sought to fill it.

He pitied them in his magnanimous moments, and cursed them in his dark ones, but mostly he feared them for what they could do to the world with their wealth and power, a destruction they'd already wrought upon themselves. Fateful irony that: to love yourself so much you destroy yourself. A dead end and slow suicide. Why couldn't they see? Narcissism had always been the same, back to very Narcissus himself. With science's plethora of vaunted new knowledge, as the specialists deem it, why could the ancient Greeks know a truth that the progressive new age did not? Chauncey had come to realize that maybe then there was no new knowledge, that knowledge was and has always been one. The store of facts could be increased, but knowledge could not. It could only shrink and be lost if one were not careful. He feared that the careless ones of his time had done just that.

Chauncey felt how simple and natural the creative act, but how complicated too. What one created was the sum total of all his accumulated experiences, and of just who he was, and that involved all those who'd gone before. Open the channels, focus, feel, delve, plough deep and turn up unused fallow soil, plant properly with good seed stock, tend and protect vigilantly, sacrifice if necessary in order to do so, and let the words grow into their orderly fields. The miracle of it, he thought. Just as some unknown life energy got into the germinating seed, so it was to Chauncey in the mind of man.

On a blank sheet he now wrote a single line in his neat pen. The black ink shown startlingly against the white: **GREED IS THE RESORT OF THE UNINSPIRED.**

Chauncey looked to his fields. He felt connected to the life force here as he could never do on the paved street. That particular trip to the city with Trig kept returning to him, putting into stark relief all that he valued and loved and what he did not.

He closed his eyes and let his mind play over his patchwork quilt landscape of fields, pastures, hills, creeks, and woods, imaging it as through the sharp eyes of a red-tailed hawk soaring high with the wind currents. He was half in a doze. Startled by the cry of the actual bird, he opened his eyes to see the landscape sharply etched as he'd never seen it before. The bird's call had that lovely plaintive sound he could never quite describe. His windows and doors were open and he could hear the cries clear. To him it was the sound that best captured the place. If he could get that on paper, he could leave the world satisfied.

Then he could see the bird. It was getting dark across the tree line and hills now, but the hawk caught the rays of the sun, high up as it was. It was a golden bird lit that way, maybe even a bird of Byzantium, but not of Yeats's beaten gold of artifice. It was not an object of art, but the real bird, and as the land grew into deeper shadow, it flashed burnished bronze before it disappeared, illuminated by the setting sun's last rays. Yes, the artifice of eternity, Chauncey thought, the immutable perfect thing frozen in the mind like the marble frieze on Keats's urn. Chauncey took the rhythms of Billy's "French Broad" and the image of the golden bird with him that night into sleep and they never really left his inner being from that time.

Five

NEXT DAY, CHAUNCEY was still reflecting on his and Trig's trip. He remembered how, heading back from Spartanburg, they'd passed through a quiet landscape of small farms, patches of woodland, cool springs and deep ravines and thicknesses where fern-lined streams ran over ledges of rock. Chauncey slowed and looked at the whitewater shoals of the Enoree. The water flowing over the rocks had a soothing sound.

He took the long way, enjoying the drive. They both did, and they'd sat silent. Occasionally Trig would have to spit in his cup, but after so many days of pain, the tooth wasn't hurting him. What a great relief, and he once again felt at ease.

An airliner had passed overhead, probably on one of its routes from Atlanta to Greenville-Spartanburg. It was flying low, already in its trajectory of descent, and made a racket. The cows in one of the fields chewed on as if nothing was going on.

Trig commented that he'd never been in a jet and didn't expect he ever would. He paused as he thought for a moment. "Pa always said people shouldn't ever go higher than corn grows or lower than you plant sweet potatoes. He didn't even like to climb a ladder to paint the second storey of our house. And I'm a lot like him."

Chauncey declared he found some wisdom in what Trig's pa said.

Then Chauncey entertained his friend with a story he's heard about one of their distant Clay Bank County cousins. Seems he had a pressing reason to fly somewhere or other, but was so devoted to his Labrador that he wouldn't leave him to do it. His family insisted, so he made up a story to airline officials that he was blind and that his inseparable companion was a seeing-eye dog. It worked, and he flew. Trig considered that a capital tale.

On their ride, Chauncey and Trig had looked at newly ploughed fields and the blood red hills against the bright blue winter sky. Chauncey was conscious that north of Spartanburg the blue mountains rose in their silent ancient wall. He knew that here where they drove southward, the billows of the old Cotton South broke against the shores of the Land of the Sky.

They'd passed Mount Pisgah Church, with a message on its changeable board: **I WILL LIFT MINE EYES UNTO THE HILLS WHENCE COMETH MY STRENGTH**. Some of the characters were missing. Apparently the **N**'s and T's had been in short supply, but the meaning came through just the same.

No, the two friends weren't calling on the mountains, like General Morgan did of old. In fact, they had their backs to the mountains and were returning to their own hills. In Chauncey's mind, they were fighting another kind of desperate war, with more than rivers at their backs.

Today Chauncey reflected upon how so much had changed since that drive to Spartanburg. Clint was married and Ida Jessine had a baby on the way. As Farmer Lyman put it in the language of the old time, she was wearing her apron high.

Kildee's daughter had also got married, and Kildee had helped her and her new husband set up house on a nearby farm. This left only one child at home with him and Lula Bess, and to both their surprise, she'd just got engaged. Kat was nineteen. She was awfully young, Lula Bess thought, but then she remembered she'd gotten married to Kildee at just her age.

Two months ago, Farmer Lyman had died of pneumonia. The doctors had found he had cancer in its advanced stages, metastasised in the bones, so they all felt that pneumonia was a kinder way to go. "The old person's friend," the doctor had called it. He'd died without much suffering, his grandchildren by his side. Annalee and Dinah were taking it hard.

They all missed him at the store. The men never ceased to bring him into their conversations, however, with "As old Mr. Lyman put it" or "As old Mr. Lyman use to say." Lyman wasn't there in person, but his words and the keen memory of him were.

Kildee, after what might have been called a close call, was still running the country store and seemed to be more contented now the decision to keep it open was made. He'd come back to acting like his old self.

Back in June, Spurgeon Adams had a stroke. He was walking across his yard in his usual rush, and about to climb the steps to his house, when he crumpled down. Lucky Mrs. Adams was at home and saw him fall. They'd airlifted him to Columbia from Clay Bank County Hospital, and after a big operation and a week in intensive care, he'd survived. Kildee, Chauncey, and Trig had visited him there. Clint drove Chauncey down twice. On the way home, the two marvelled at all the tubes all over their friend. They reminded Clint of a great spider web. The men declared that this time they bet Spurgeon would slow down and stay mostly still. The great spider called medicine had got him in its web. His doctor's assessment was that the operation was successful and the outlook was good. Spurgeon said that the operation had to be a triumph because the entire contents of his wallet were successfully removed. In talking, he slightly slurred some of his words. Mrs. Adams told Kildee this was likely going to be permanent, but she thanked the Lord his movements wouldn't be impaired.

On the first drive home from Columbia, Clint and Chauncey had had the chance to talk openly alone for the first time in months. Clint could tell Chauncey how happy he was in his marriage to Ida Jessine. "And, man, the sex is good!" he'd declared before he'd thought. Once he realised what he'd said, the colour rose in his face. At that, Chauncey laughed a little, and said, “Well. Well.” He figured both Clint and Ida were virgins when they wed, but had no trouble with taking right off to married folks ways. She’d gotten pregnant straight away and her due time would be almost nine months to the day after their wedding. They saw no reason to wait to have a child. They weren’t wealthy, but God would provide. They didn’t have self-actualisation, finding themselves, or careers to put ahead. “First things first,” Clint had said.

Lula Bess’s cousin Dana was moving back to Clay Bank. Lula Bess had prevailed, and now Kildee had found her an old abandoned farmhouse. As run down as the Ben Sims Place was, it was affordable, and several in the community were helping her to make the place livable. Chauncey and Trig were among the crew. Were it not for just having to set up his own household, Clint would have also pitched in in a big way.

Kildee figured that with the right assistance, Dana might even put some of the fields back in tillage once again. The farm had been a good one in its day. And the soil lying fallow now for more than a decade, would be extra rich. “Itching for seed," he'd said. "Planting might be dangerous. It'd be like the story of the old sow that stole an ear of corn and slept on a few grains. The old folks said that the percussion of the sprouting kernels killed her dead. Be careful with planting in that rich soil, Miss Dana," he said. "This year when I planted okra seed in my fallow land, the sound it made coming up was like popping corn in an aluminum pan."

Dana Lee Oxner and Chauncey were born in the same year. They'd been in school together for twelve years and graduated at the same time. When she'd gone off to college, got married, and took her job in Charlotte, Chauncey soon lost track of her. He'd left Clay Bank too, and she seldom visited home, and when she did, he wasn't there. Their paths never crossed. He'd nearly put her out of his mind, like something treasured you'd place in the back of a drawer and then forgot. But now, as his neighbour and a close friend of Lula Bess, she was squarely back in his life.

Dana was pretty. She'd taken good care of herself. In Charlotte, she jogged and worked out at a fitness salon. She'd always taken pride in the way she looked and now already took part in the womanly ritual of the area in going every Friday to Classy Cuts, the beauty salon one of Lula Bess's cousins operated in the converted double garage next to her house. It was Friday of course to look good for church on Sunday.

Now Chauncey and Dana saw each other every day or so. When they did, he'd usually have a hammer or saw in his hand, helping her make repairs. And if he was working at the appropriate time, she'd serve him a meal in the big comfortable kitchen of the farm house. Bess was teaching her how to fix "comfort foods," as Dana called them, the dishes she'd loved as a child and that reminded her of old times: sage seasoned dressing with the baked hen, corn bread, cheese pie, rice and gravy with the fried chicken, fried okra and squash. Then the desserts! Japanese fruit cake with ambrosia, banana pudding, sweet potato casserole, coconut cake, pecan pie. Chauncey and she both loved sweets.

Cousin Bess was probably the happiest to have her girlhood friend back home. She had her over to the house for supper several times a week and for Sunday dinner after church at one o'clock. At church, they sat in the same group of pews, sharing space with Kildee and five of Bess's children, their husbands and wives, and their growing, more or less well-behaved, young brood.

Dana loved the closeness there, and felt how lucky she was to be included. She knew she'd been gathered in, and she'd not had this feeling since her first few years of marriage before everything started going wrong. She began speaking of the congregation as her church family.

Dana told Lula Bess about city life as she'd lived it. She said the ultra-rich made poor neighbours, if neighbours you could call them at all. She unburdened herself in a great burst: "They like to show they can afford to be somewhere else. That's their new game. They're always on a cruise or jetting to some distant point on the globe. They've got several houses here and there, and the houses are all so wonderful that each demands a visit, and that leaves empty ones next to you. Get enough of them and it's like Wall Street after dark."

Lula Bess had heard tell of such places. She refused to call them neighbourhoods. "Sounds like the meaning of ultra-rich is absence," she said.

"Abuse, more like." After a pause, Dana concluded with a bit of unaccustomed drama, "Their heaps of money buy them a new kind of poverty."

Lula Bess made a point of often including Chauncey at meals. He'd been a Sunday dinner regular before Dana returned, but now he was there sometimes during the week for supper as well. About this, Lula Bess, in her knowing way, was pleased as punch.

When Trig was around Chauncey and Dana, he always smiled knowingly, but didn't say a word.

In all the flux of the last two years, it was only Trig who hadn't changed. Chauncey saw him as a kind of North Star, always steady in the sky to set the tiller of your rudder by, and someone he could always count on. He was the same old Trig. Not a care in the world. He still walked ramrod straight with his youthful long stride. His thick shock of coppery hair only showed grey at the ears. Chauncey's head now was almost fully white. He'd thought recently about using a Grecian Formula hair dye, but decided he'd not. Kildee and Trig probably would have ragged him hard if he had. He figured dark hair wasn't worth it, considering that.

Dana was often on his mind. "You Eustacia. Me Wildeve," he thought with a wry smile, echoing the "Me Tarzan. You Jane" of the little of Hollywood he knew as a child. "Only this Eustacia had gotten away and didn't like where she'd gotten to. One native had already returned before the other one did, and neither had stayed home to be returned to. A thoroughly modern scenario. It would make better than the usual Keith Urban song."

Yes. And after two years, and checking out of rehab, Keith Urban was still married to Nicole.

"Will wonders never cease!" Chauncey muttered. He thought about Dana's own failed marriage and divorce, how the son had gone with the father and how Billy was now grown up and off on his own.

Change and more change this last year. Ten months ago, Dana's ex-husband Greg Somerset had died in a big car wreck near Durham. He was in his BMW Roadster. The police report showed alcohol. He'd swerved over the white line and hit head on and at a pretty high speed. The other driver and his family were in an S. U. V. and had come away with some bad bruises and cuts, but hadn't been killed. One child's head had hit the windshield, but after a week had been released from the hospital, as the doctors said, as good as new.

Billy was taking his father's death hard. After she and Greg had split fifteen years ago, the lad, who was ten at the time, had chosen to be with his dad. She and her son, while seeing each other frequently enough after that, were not close. When they met, there was always a kind of formality between them, occasioned by hurt on both sides.

She'd reached out to him after Greg died. They sat next to each other through the funeral service and found comfort in each other throughout the ordeal.

But Greg and Billy were Somersets, and she'd taken back her maiden name. For Chauncey, that about said it all.

Billy Somerset was about to turn twenty-five. He'd graduated with honours from the University at Chapel Hill. He had what the world deemed a good money-making degree. Clint would have called it a tech school certificate. Now, he had a high-paying job as a chemical engineer at the Research Triangle outside Raleigh.

Dana learned that Allison, the woman he'd gotten serious about, worked down the hall at a lab in the same office building. She was an N. C. State alum and was six years older. She'd been working there since 1999, and made almost twice his salary. She was part of what Dana called the Triangle's Bastion of Bourgeois Bohemians, a B triangle itself, a realm of rootless, ambitious, and bright new careerists who did all the trendy liberalish things. Dana had to deal with their type a lot in her job and knew their sort well. In some ways, they reminded her of herself when she'd first come to Charlotte, but without her innocence. They'd already developed a kind of cynical world-weariness which they and much of the world took for sophistication. Most of the associates with whom Allison socialised lived in nearby Cary. There, they'd made their own insulated make-believe world. Allison had just recently moved there too. Most of her friends were young marrieds, and she thought she'd like to be like them and enter fully into their life style. Billy was presentable and could play the role. In a lot of ways, he was made to order for the situation, ideal. If there were any square edges to his peg, she felt she could round them off. As for

Billy himself, although he hadn't thought about it much, he seemed ready enough to surrender his edges and fit in.

Last month, Dana learned that Billy had given Allison a ring. She'd accepted his proposal and they'd set a date for later this year. Dana was happy for Billy and wished she'd learned of his engagement from him and not a mutual friend. The coolness was still there. His marriage would take something of a load off her mind.

Dana had met Allison only twice, once at a party in Raleigh, and then at Greg's funeral.

She'd helped Billy with the funeral arrangements. Dana wasn't asked.

Dana liked her well enough. She seemed a lot more worldly wise, mature, and self-assured than Billy. "Executive," was Dana's word to describe her. "Executive in a good way," she'd add. Allison seemed to be mothering him. "Well, whatever floats your boat," Dana said.

It was Billy's choice, not hers. He'd not asked her advice and she'd not volunteered. The death of his father had seemed to speed things along. Greg had approved of Allison, and who was she to chime in? In the thoroughly modern way, Billy said he wasn't marrying her family, and

Allison wasn't marrying what was left of his.

Allison's folks were from Illinois and he'd met them only once. She'd come to North Carolina on a university scholarship and had gone home only infrequently herself. With her scholarship and a good part time job, she'd been financially independent even while a student. At thirty-one, she hadn't married and didn't have kids. "No baggage there," Dana felt and was relieved. She wished them well. She'd only enter their lives as much and in ways that they wanted her to.

Just last week, Billy had called and given her his new address and cell phone number. He'd moved into Allison's condo in Cary. In the background, Dana could hear a loud buzzing sound. It was Allison's exer-cycle, Billy said.

So with Billy about to be married, Dana was truly on her own now. She had the fewest responsibilities she'd had in years. With her very new life, which was so familiarly the old one, maybe she'd heal wounds she didn't even fully realise she had.

Six

A FEW DAYS LATER, one of Trig's neighbours dropped him off at Chauncey's for a short visit. It was late afternoon; Chauncey had finished his chores and had a little time to write. As he sat down, he recalled William Blake in his readings a few weeks ago, something to the effect that it was in the second which Satan spared the poet, that his work is done. He looked at the empty page. The words weren't coming and he was glad for Trig's visit.

"Well, Chaunts, so the well's dry."

"Seems it is."

After half hour's catching up on the events of the past week since they'd seen each other, they concluded that, all things considered, it was a good week—not having much going on. They were both glad they were off the beaten track of what the world calls progress, where things happen so swiftly your head swims.

Chauncey had about concluded that his people were smart in not running breathlessly after fads. He understood well what Farmer Lyman meant when he declared, "Our people don't embrace change; they bear it!" Not having earth-shattering events didn't bother Chauncey at all. He liked his small circle of acquaintances and friends. He'd learned that when individuals are few, each one counts for more and people are not desensitized into abstractions. Or so he was always mumbling to himself.

He remembered in detail his and Lyman's conversation that day, one of the last they'd had before the old man died. Chauncey had just run across a quotation from Oscar Wilde that he passed on to his friend: "Fashion is creating something so intolerable that it has to be changed every six months." That had given Mr Lyman a chuckle, and, now, especially, Chauncey was real glad of it.

Today, the talk had turned to the new technical era. Chauncey explained to Trig how Dana, accustomed to the world of Charlotte offices, had told him he needed to get a computer for his writing. "Would make your life a lot easier," she said. The old way of calling it was "word processing," but Chauncey didn't want to process words. It reminded him of Velveeta cheese. He preferred the hand-cut savory richly-coloured hoop variety at Kildee's store. If he had to prune verbiage, he wanted to use his hands and not electric hedge trimmers or a weed eater. Yesterday she was telling him about a new Apple.

"She sounds like Eve to me," Trig ventured after a while.

"Now I know how Adam felt," Chauncey replied. He had seen the large red Apple computer logo in Columbia on a billboard, a silhouette apple with a big bite taken out of its right side. He explained it to his friend, who was amazed. Chauncey had also heard recent talk by psychologists who were wondering about the long term effects of the new technology on the very young by refiguring the brain.

"Well, there's that apple with the bite taken out," Trig said. "Seems the devil's given fair warning as he usually does with such leaps and we're so willful we refuse to see. Bet Old Scratch is shaking with laugher to the end of his forked tail."

"It's not like we don't have the warnings from all such fast leaps in the past, that with one advance, there'd be two steps back, and faith that there'd be new technology to come to undo the bad effects of the old," Chauncey added. "And now Dana wants me on e-mail and to get a cell phone."

To this, Trig replied after a pause, "I've seen all them people in town, on the streets, even in their cars, talking to these little things at their ear. Look like crumpled up little bats. I call 'em electronic dog leashes. And this thing called the Web that Dana was telling me about that you'll have if she can persuade you to get a computer. Well, Chauncey, you know what sits in a web. There he sits, waiting. You jiggle your little corner and the whole thing shakes, and then it is that he pounces. I've always pitied that fly. Little chance he has."

These new advances were leaps indeed. Chauncey recalled Lyman's response when he'd ventured that the automobile had been a bad influence and weakened community. "I'm still not reconciled to the wheel," he said, and after a while added, "And them that debated the flat earth and round earth ways of seeing the world. If the old flat earth way had won out, and folks would have been scared of falling off the rim, they'd at least think twice before leaving home."

Chauncey remembered that conversation with a wistful smile. He missed his friend.

He looked over at Trig, who'd noticed his expression as it turned from wistful to playful. "Guess I'm just a trogluddite," Chauncey ventured.

"A what?"

Since he got no answer, Trig said after a quiet interval, "Well Chaunts, it won't be long before supper time. Harold will be honking that horn to take me home. Fine too. My mind's turning to food."

Chauncey offered to get his friend a ham biscuit from the warming closet, but Trig declined. He had fried ham, half an iron skillet of corn bread and the pot-likker from a big mess of turnip and mustard greens waiting for him on the old stove at home.

Chauncey's eye rested a split second on the blank page. As usual, his friend caught his mood.

"Sorry about what you call 'block.' Maybe you ought to try Fleet. You do know the two meanings of Fleet, don't you?"

"Well, maybe...Actually, no." Chauncey pleaded ignorance, reckoning there'd be an original take on the word, and so it was.

"*Fleet*, it means quick, and I reckon it is; and a fleet is a *lot* of ships, one letter off."

In the distance, Harold's truck motor could be heard as he turned onto Chauncey's clay lane.

"Well, here you go," Trig said standing and looking serious. "Take this down on your pretty lined paper with that fancy silver dip pen, a pome by Trig T. My stomach's growling for home."

Harold's truck engine had idled and stopped. Trig went on, "Careful now. Get every word. They's golden."

POT-LIKKER
drink it
dunk it
sop it
want it—now!

He reached the door in one long stride, then paused, turned, and said, ""Chaunts, you know all that about the sun and moon and stars? Well, they just are."

And the screen door slammed behind him at the same time the horn tooted and before his friend could say bye.

Chauncey sat thinking as the motor droned down the lane to the highway. "Well, well, well.

They just are. No ideas but in things. Old Trig's an Imagist. Or has he gone one step further?" He thought of Trig and Wallace Stevens or Amy Lowell sharing corn bread and pot-likker and discussing the art of poetry. He chuckled to himself as he closed his notebook and put down his pen.

"No following that today," he said to Mowdie as she arched her back and rubbed against the leg of his chair. She had absented herself while Trig was there, knowing, as she did, his rambunctiousness. With his leaving, she had now quietly reappeared. "Think I'll go out and plant that yellowwood seedling that's getting pot bound." Mowdie looked at him as if she might have intuited his mood.

As he put on his heavier shoes for digging, he thought, *Cladrastis lutea*, *Cladrastis kentukea*. He wished the horticulturists would quit changing its name. "*Virgilia*," he said the old name aloud with some conviction. He liked the connection of the tree to the poet he loved. He thought of the Cherokee using the new shoots for yellow dye and could see in his mind's eye the clusters of cream and white flowers that dripped luxuriantly beautiful from its branches just every other spring. It was a tricky tree to start from seed. They took two years to germinate. Chauncey remembered the day he planted this little sapling's seed and the things going on in his life at the time. Now, a time ahead, he would likely recall the day he planted it. That's how he planted and farmed. His land was a wide remembrance garden. He had no real need for a diary or log, though he kept one, mainly for the discipline and the need to communicate in his often solitary world.

He caught the screen door as it was about to slam. He always recollected his grandfather's saying that if you let a screen door slam, it caught a ghost in it, and that was certainly not a good thing. Chauncey had read somewhere that this was an old Irish superstition but wondered if it just wasn't a way to stop that irritating sound, particularly with a lot of young'uns running around. He didn't like it either and envisioned ghosts quietly inhabiting his same space and for whom he was being considerate. How would it feel to be trapped in a door?

Bergamot his beagle came out from under the porch to sniff the cat and promptly got a warning that he heeded straightway. He followed his master as he headed for the barn to get his planting shovel. There was still plenty of daylight left in this glorious clear day and Chauncey decided he was going to make the best of it. There were also a couple of seedling buckeyes he'd grown in pots. He'd get them in the ground as well.

"*Aesculus pavia, Aesculus parviflora, Aesculus octandra, Aesculus splendens, Aesculus sylvatica, Aesculus lutea,*" he said in a kind of chant that he adapted to the rhythm of his stride as he went barn-ward. "*Life is good. And all living things feel it,*" the sunshine seemed to say as it touched his face. The sun was including him in that, and he felt one with the world. He was seeing the long graceful white plumes of the bottlebrush buckeye as he opened the door to the barn's dark world.

Seven

CHAUNCEY NO LONGER called Dana a divorcee. She was now officially a widow, and this made a difference to him.

He'd had a friend in Georgia who was involved with a divorced woman whose ex-husband was very much alive. The woman was pushing hard for marriage, but his friend was resisting. Chauncey remembered him saying, "Adultery. Chauncey, is it worth breaking the commandment and losing my soul for?" The friend, who read his King James every night before going to bed took Scripture at its word. As long as the husband survived, divorce or no, remarriage was adultery. The friend had said he was beginning to put more and more stock in the words written in red. And the red-letter words were not subject to interpretation on this point. "Where God puts a period, you don't substitute a comma," he'd said.

Chauncey and Trig had talked about this some months ago. Trig had commented that no preacher he knew today would get close to the subject of adultery, wouldn't touch it with a ten-foot pole.

"But still the word in Scripture is clear," Chauncey had replied. "There's no exception, no hedging there. And it's there in red. But as many times as I've been to church, I've never heard that passage read."

"I expect in a lot of places there wouldn't be a congregation left if the preacher did," Trig continued. "With half of the marriages failing and remarryings again and again as casual as the leaf falls, whatever seems convenient rules. And that-there ex-congregation would just move somewhere else across town where they could keep on feeling good. Nobody wants to hear things that will keep them from doing what they want to. *Me, My, Mine.* It's a *Me*-centred world."

Chauncey had thought awhile and replied, "You're right, Trig. Nowadays preachers can't inconvenience congregations and make them feel bad. That's the worse sin. Wonder what the old prophets would have said."

"Don't need to wonder," Trig picked up the thread. "Somebody like Jeremiah or Daniel or Amos, and Ezekiel. All gristle and backbone and not needing the collection plate to build a new family life centre to keep up with the rival mega-church across town."

Family life centre. Chauncey was struck for the first time with the irony of the word. How could there be family, centred or otherwise, with split families, splitting in chain reaction like atoms in a kind of social atomic bomb.

The statistic of one out of two marriages failing haunted him. This was nationwide. In the South, it wasn't that high. In South Carolina, lower still, but high enough. In Clay Bank County, until recently, split families weren't heard of at all. In his neighbourhood, he knew of only one.

But he also knew that his region and state, even his county were just behind the times. With the years, they'd no doubt catch up and join in. Unless some divine intervention occurred.

"A family life centre," he'd said again. "There can't be life unless the centre holds."

So here Chauncey sat again today in his big overstuffed chair in his little reading alcove, thinking of the folly of men.

He reached to the shelves behind him, and took down his well-thumbed copy of Yeats. He knew the words by heart, but he wanted to see them once again there on the printed page. *Turning and turning in the widening gyre, the falcon cannot hear the falconer...Things fall apart...the blood-dimmed tide is loosed...the centre cannot hold.*

Studying Yeats closely as he had over the years, Chauncey figured he knew what the poet had meant by his rough rude beast of the new way. For Yeats, this creature with the pitiless gaze slouching toward Bethlehem to be born must have been the unfeeling animal offspring of Industry, Science and Socialism, the new power and machine worshiping gods of the world. These new idols collided, as all material philosophies must, with the words written in red. Chauncey felt that the raw new words of power were also written in red, the scarlet of a blood-letting time that had brought on a hundred years of war and environmental disaster.

He breathed with several quick bursts through his nose, forcing air into his blocked sinuses. He adjusted the glasses on his eyes. "Slouching towards Bethlehem," he said. "Moving on its slow thighs, shadowed by indignant desert birds."

He paused and stared blankly at the page. "The Morrigan," he said aloud. "Picking at the flesh of the slain. The darkness drops again. Wars and rumours of war. A blood-dyed century. Amazons of blood. The west intent on suicide."

After a while, he looked up from his book and out his alcove window to his fields, dark with the blades of corn. "Green shuck time," old Mr Lyman called this time of the year, as did the people of old. Time for pulling roastin'ears.

Chauncey thought back nearly two years ago when he'd heard on the news that Nazareth was being bombed by fatal rockets unleashed from Lebanon. Nazareth in Judea, the very home of the Prince of Peace was feeling the rude beast's tread. The Socialists in Tel Aviv had bombed Beirut and now the bombed ones were defending themselves, bombing back in turn. It was a crazy world of upward spiraling retaliations, another blood-dimmed tide unleashed on the battered, already beaten-up world.

Chauncey considered how few in the world heeded the words of *Ephesians*: "Proclaim the gospel of peace. Take the shield of faith to quench the fiery darts of the evil one." He knew that the words of Scripture used the military language of the Roman Empire in the first century. He felt how similar was the world's situation today when empires and the dire consequences of empires still shadowed the earth. He was saddened that the United States was now one of these unleashing the red tide, killing the old and women and children he would never know, creating orphans and widows and countless refugees who would never find a home.

And now Yeats's beast would soon be a century old, or was he still just being born, his rocking cradle vexing all to nightmare. If the latter, what would the grown beast be? Even with his fertile imagination, Chauncey couldn't imagine such a terrible thing. When he looked down again, he was surprised to find tears on his page.

The insane folly of man.

His mind turned to his own land. The march of the beast had begun in February 1865, when an invading army 50,000 strong, had put everything to the torch. His father had passed down stories of that time that he'd heard from his own pa.

And then after that war, the burning had not stopped. Chauncey recalled Clint's figures from college. His professor had studied the loss of the Southern forests to Northern capitalists from 1865 into the twentieth century. He'd been amazed to hear that 149,000,000 acres of Southern forest had been clear-cut and hauled away on trains built by the robber baron elite. At 640 acres per square mile, that amounted to more than 233,000 square miles. When he'd looked up the size of states and found that this area was larger than South Carolina, Georgia, Alabama, and Mississippi combined, his mouth had dropped open in amazement. There had been a verdant forested land, but only a few vestiges of old growth remained in his state—Congaree and Beidler Forest by name. He had visited them a decade ago and those visits had helped place him on the path he took today.

Clint's description of the absentee owners' practise of firing the mounds of debris left from the clear-cutting haunted his mind. Clint's prof had said these piles were often five stories high and sometimes smouldered for two years. All across the South they burned. And as the South burned, those responsible were feverishly building cities and factories, paving the world, and amassing great piles of gold. *Converting green into gold,* he thought. This was a double curse to the earth. Loving trees the way he did, the thought of this was almost too much for him to bear.

Chauncey reflected that his agrarian culture was not responsible for climate change and the global environmental crisis. It was by its very nature "green." Like the English gentry who lived on and valued the land, his planter ancestors had resisted urbanisation and factories. Chauncey knew global warming to be a reality and that the tipping point was approaching if it hadn't already been reached—the point when there wasn't anything anyone could do to reverse matters. His look into the horizon of the future saw the heated seas releasing methane gas that would bubble to the surface and burn—a sea of flame that would only accelerate the end. This spectre came to him often. He knew that the final result would be a planet that would no longer sustain human life. He'd heard cockroaches could withstand the radiation of nuclear blast, but he figured even they couldn't survive this. In all his fright, anger, and sadness, he at least took some satisfaction knowing that his own ancestors hadn't brought on the end, and in fact had died trying to defend their farming way of life.

"Enough of this," he said to the calico cat

lapping cream from her bowl at the screen door. She looked up at him with gentle large eyes of thanks as she continued to drink with her delicate pink tongue. It flicked out so quickly you could hardly see. Chauncey knew cat nature. Most of them seemed indifferent to anything having to do with man. They were certainly usually flatly indifferent to gifts; they acted as if they were above gifts in fact, and were aloof from the world.

But he could tell that this one comprehended she had good reason for thanks. She was somebody's throwaway. Somebody from city or town dumped her tiny form out here by his country road. Or maybe she was a feral animal born out in the woods from an earlier dumped one. She'd crawled onto his porch near starved. Circling buzzards revealed two of her litter down the road being recycled into buzzards. She had herself been a few hours from death and had only come to his house out of extremity. Chauncey knew it would have taken this, for she so feared man. "It's either you I don't know and whom I fear with all my quaking heart, or certain death and buzzards," she'd reasoned in her cat brain. It took several weeks for her not to sneak timidly onto the porch for food. Chauncey knew it was surely out of desperation that she'd come the first time, and with her last ounce of strength, approached that forked creature called man.

Man's cruelty to the helpless still never ceased to amaze Chauncey.

The cat finished her cream and he watched her walk down the steps and out into the yard. She sat for a moment with her long tail curled neatly and beautifully covering her front paws. She watched him back with some interest, seeing what he'd be up to. She trusted him now and would wait on the porch in morning and evening, sometimes meowing for food. He called her Mowdie, in imitation of the sound she made.

She knew she'd found her a home and in her dignified, stately, and self-contained way, declared the place hers, but also that she'd decided to share it with him.

Chauncey smiled at that, got up, and refilled the bowl. He'd trained his beagles and Walkers that this bowl was off limits and good-naturedly they more or less obeyed. They, his beagle, his two setters, his Boykin, Mowdie the calico, and his three other cats, had made a diplomatic truce.

Chauncey studied how these and the farm animals negotiated space, compromised, and got along. They seemed to keep a matter-of-fact practicality and even something that amounted to a sense of humour about it all.

"Why can't us women and men?" he asked his face in the mirror as he combed his hair. He then put on his light jacket, a recent Christmas present from Lula Bess and Kildee. He got his wallet and his truck keys. He'd decided he'd go over to Dana's to see if she needed help with her chores.

Eight

CHAUNCEY FOUND DANA hanging clothes on the line. She wore a thin, flowered print dress with an old-fashioned ruffled apron tied at the waist. She hadn't noticed him come down the lane, or she'd have turned to greet him. The breeze blew the hem of her dress into motion.

He didn't announce his presence just yet, but instead paused, enjoying the sight of her at her chore. He could hear she was humming a song but couldn't tell what.

The clothes shone in the sun and whipped in the breeze. He'd made the clothes line himself, getting Clint's brother Chris to weld the cross bar arms to three sturdy iron posts. He'd figured two sections, each twenty feet long, of three rows of wires would take care of her needs. There'd be no diapers, and clothes for only one. He used his own line as model. As he paused watching Dana, he reckoned he'd allowed right.

She had a clothes pin bag slung over her neck. It hung to her left side. Nolee May, Chris's wife, had made it for her when Dana had commented on how handy Nolee May's looked. Nolee May was Lula Bess's oldest daughter, and she and Chris were her closest neighbours to the north.

Occasionally, she'd put a pin in her teeth to free both hands. Chauncey observed that she had her own way of hanging clothes. She hung the shirts and blouses by their collars and not by their tails and hems like most women did around here. She pinned her slacks by the cuffs and not the waist bands. Everything was backwards, but she was getting the job done just the same.

In Charlotte, she'd had the regulation washer and dryer in a special laundry room next to the mud room and garage. Like everybody in her neighbourhood. "Funny thing about the mud room," she now thought, "there was never any mud. Everything was either manicured grass or paved." "Tidy" was the optimum word. She never realised the irony in the mud room when she lived there. It took coming here to see. "That world was so regulated in all the things that didn't matter, and what needed it was chaos," she now concluded. "Everything had to be intersecting at right angles, so neat and proper, so it seemed. It was like a template placed on life, but the template ended up replacing it, with nothing left inside." She'd finally got fed up with the meaningless routine.

This hanging out clothes to dry in the sun of a Monday was a new thing for her. The uninitiated may have felt this to be a tiresome routine, but she knew it as ritual and a joyful one at that. It meant she was home. Her mama had done it, but she never had before. It took more work, but "Gee," she'd told Lula Bess the other day, "Don't the clothes smell good. Especially the sheets. I'd forgotten how great fresh clothes smell. I love to fold them when I take them inside. Fresh sheets on the bed are one of the little pleasures of the world. I bought a lot of things in Charlotte, all those expensive perfumes and lavender scented linen sprays, sprays to make the sheets and clothes smell fresh and seem that they'd hung in the sun. But now I can judge they didn't at all. How simple it is to get that smell from just using the sunshine and not something bottled by men."

"It seems y'all paid so much for what was just outside," Bess had replied. She'd thought but didn't say, "That's what happens in a world where people try to make everything into what can be bought and sold."

Dana had compromised in the washing category when she'd set up her new household. She had the Mayflower moving van bring her washer, but sold the dryer at a mammoth yard sale. She figured she wasn't going to pound clothes on river rocks or get washboard and washtub, but she could hang clothes on the line. She didn't have a five day work schedule now. She'd wash clothes on Monday, weather permitting, as the women around here did still. If it looked rainy, she'd wait until a day when the sky cleared. This was another way she'd work with nature and not separate from it via machine.

She told Chauncey, "All this business about environment. Environment this, and environment that. Global warming this and global warming that. I agree we're at the point of crisis, but instead of talk, people could save so much electricity just by hanging out clothes."

Clint, who'd overheard the conversation, and remembering a few of the official stats he'd learned at college from an elaborate study of how peeing outside instead of flushing commodes would save billions of gallons of water each year, commented that he wondered what professor would get a fat government grant to prove the obvious again. He could hear the scholarly paper now: "Tumble Dry Versus the Vertical: A Statistical Theory of Open-Air Clothes Drying Techniques." The title was perfect. It even had the obligatory colon.

Dana and Chauncey laughed.

"You missed your calling," Dana told him. "You'd be good in that college world. Ex-farm boys usually are. They theorise in order to get off the farm and keep from having to go back."

"Not this ol' farm boy," he'd said. "Just the reverse. Got out quick as I could and used that paper vet's degree as a ticket home."

Dana had worked in the regional headquarters of a great timber and paper company mega-concern. She was the executive secretary and aide to the CEO, and had seen so many studies like that on staff members' desks. But she didn't have anything new to tell him because he'd gotten his vet degree from a school that had an ag department and he'd taken a lot of classes there.

"Mornin' Dana," Chauncey said at last. She recognised his voice and turned with a smile.

She straightened a wisp of hair the wind had freed from its place and that had fallen over her brow. A hand went automatically to her hip, where she smoothed her dress.

"You ought to wear a hat. Out here in the sun. It's got some real sting even this time of year."

He took his ball cap off and put it on her head. The mottled camo tan of its design looked right on her auburn hair. It had an embroidered Levi Garrett patch on its front.

She raised her face up to him and gave his cheek the brush of a kiss.

"Well, what did I do to deserve that?" he asked.

Dana didn't answer. She was busy placing sheets on the line. Wet as they were, they were heavy and awkward to handle, "bunglesome," Lula Bess would have said. So Chauncey helped her string and pin them up. They were soft, fancy sheets, part of her designer bedroom in that other world. Chauncey liked the intimacy of helping her with them.

She put the split oak clothes basket Trig had made for her on the redwood picnic table she'd moved from her city yard. She and Chauncey sat there together, passing news back and forth, things of no great moment to the busy world.

"I came over to see if you needed any help on anything," he said. "It's lay-by time, and I got some hours to spare."

"Unless you want to mop the kitchen floor, you've got off the hook today."

He'd brought a large basket of apples he'd picked from his grandmother's trees. They weren't perfect and waxed to a shine, but they made up for looks in taste. Their little freckled blemishes advertised that they were poison free.

"They're beautiful. They smell so good. Thanks, Chaunts," she said. "With Aunt Bessie Caldwell's help up in Flat Rock, I've learned to make a pretty good pie. I'll make you one when I make mine."

"Much obliged," Chauncey said.

They sat there quiet for a time, the autumn sun hot on their backs. It felt good to Chauncey. His muscles had been exercised a lot lately cutting up the winter wood. He was a little relieved that Dana had put in a heating system in the old house and insulated the walls. She'd drawn the line with vinyl siding though. "If I wanted to live hermetically sealed in a plastic bag, I'd stayed in town," she said. Again, *compromise* was her operative word.

Chauncey knew he would have volunteered to help her with wood, so he was glad she'd be warm without his help this first winter on the farm, for, truth to tell, he already had his hands full with farming and farm chores and cutting and chopping his own.

No, he didn't have a lot of spare time. What he had was spent in reading, going to Kildee's store, and visiting Kildee and family, Clint, and Trig. Now Dana was a great addition to his world. It extended its bounds in ways he felt but couldn't exactly put into words. She went to the church he and all the Hendersons did, the church he and Hoyalene had married in.

Chauncey was going there on Sundays more regularly now. He sat by himself, thinking it best not to move in too fast on Dana's turf. She sat with the Hendersons; and with the great number of them, there wasn't any room.

There at the picnic table, the two shared another space of time, swapping news of this and that. It was getting close to one. Dana invited Chauncey to eat a sandwich with her. Yesterday, she'd made a big pitcher of sun tea. He declined dinner but accepted a glass of tea. He'd already eaten before he came.

He followed her into the kitchen.

"Tastes like Carolina sunshine," he said as he daubed at the sweat on the glass with the napkin Dana had wrapped around the glass as she handed it to him.

"Another way to let the sun's energy do things without using up electricity," she said. "And the slow brew tastes so much better too. Wonder why more people don't make tea this way."

"Sure is good," he said. He liked the way she made it so sweet it almost hurt his teeth. That's the way people did it around there. Tea meant sweet-tea and only that. Even in Charlotte she'd found it that way.

Dana had done a lot with the kitchen. Despite her urban executive lifestyle, the kitchen had always seemed more her home in Charlotte. She'd wanted Greg and Billy to eat at the kitchen table for breakfast, but Greg had always been in too big a rush getting to the office, and when Billy started school and resisted, she gave up. When the men of the house ate, it was usually something in their hands.

And Greg had always wanted to eat at nice restaurants. When they did eat supper at home, he and Billy would help their plates and sit in front of the TV. She usually sat at the table and ate alone. She usually tried to have fresh flowers there, either cut from her yard or bought at the florist section of the Harris Teeter where she shopped. She looked at them as she ate. They were her only company.

With the distance of time, she could look more objectively now at her family life. She'd made some bad choices, but at least she'd tried to make a home. In that way, she didn't have much help from Greg. When he had the luxury of time, he chose golf and the country club. He liked the food and palling around with his socio-economic set there and the big polished teakwood bar. She didn't feel so guilty now at how things had turned out.

"Greg and I came from different worlds," she'd told Chauncey the other day. He'd asked her some questions about the life they'd led. They were now close enough to talk about such things, and Chauncey could tell she needed someone to talk to.

"I thought I wanted to live in his, and just never could. I finally found out I never really did want to from the first. I didn't know what I wanted. I guess I was just confused. Greg said that to me, and I got mad. I denied it but I reckon it was true. Oh, how I remember that day. We had a real row. Billy saw it all. That night Greg slept at the house of one of his golfing buddies at the club, and next day moved out most of his clothes."

She was glad to be able to tell Chauncey of this. She'd not even been as frank and detailed with Bess. It had taken over a decade, but she'd gotten some grip on the events.

Chauncey had always been a good listener. Or so said Trig. As his father had taught him, nobody has a better control of the language than the person who can curb his tongue. This was especially hard to do, for like Trig and most of the folks around, they'd inherited the gift of blarney from the old sod.

And Chauncey really did listen, not just sit there with a vacant stare while his mind was elsewhere. Dana had picked this up about him at once.

The kitchen already had a comfortable look. She and Lula Bess had made blue-checked curtains and a matching table cloth for the old heart pine table that had been at her Grandma and Grandpa Oxner's. She'd moved it each time she moved. It had followed her on her journeys to four Charlotte homes. It was always the one constant anchor, like the hearth of a home.

Now it was back where it belonged. She figured that keeping the table was a sign she'd not really ever belonged anywhere but here. Or so it felt now. She'd successfully fooled herself for a good many years. Greg was right after all. But that dishonesty with herself was finally over and gone. At least she hoped it was. "Poor Greg," she said to Chauncey as she sat down.

Chauncey had finished his tea, and he got up to leave, but Dana stopped him. She got up too.

"You forgot something," she said.

He turned to her and looked a little puzzled. She took off his ball cap from her head and put it sideways on his.

"Come get your pie tomorrow, or if you've got too much to do, I'll bring it over."

He left his cap askew the way she'd placed it as he walked over the worn threshold.

Nine

WHEN CHAUNCEY GOT back home, he had a pleasant surprise. Clint was there in his back yard. Chauncey had left the axe sticking in the block and Clint was splitting his wood. Clint was never one to waste time and tried to make himself useful if he could.

He took Clint inside. Because he'd been waiting there for some time, he hadn't had anything to eat. The wood chopping had made him hungry. Chauncey dipped him up a big bowl of black-eyed peas and made him a quick sandwich. "Keep you from starving at least," he said.

Clint had eaten a light dinner several hours ago with Ida Jessine. She was having these strange food cravings and concocted some odd meals. Clint said he was glad to have a sandwich that didn't have mayonnaise, peanut butter, and mustard on it all at the same time. He looked at Chauncey with a look of hurt.

Chauncey had noticed that Clint had gained

weight these past months. Marriage did that to men. He felt Clint had always been a mite too thin. As tall as he was, he needed a few more pounds, and it hadn't gone to his waist. Chauncey saw he'd gained muscle too. He was probably in better shape than he'd ever been. His more or less sedentary life at college had not helped. He was certainly happier now. Farming and vetting agreed with him. Married life and being at home did too. He liked regular hours, to be able to sit down at meals at a proper time and to be able to regulate his day by the sun—to have some kind of order in his life. Still his routine was far from ideal.

He and Ida lived at the old Blair farmstead with his brother Joe-Pratt and Sallie and their four young sons. The oldest, Eppes, was eleven. Lyles was eight. Glenn was six, and little Graham had just had his second birthday. The house was full, but his brother and sister-in-law hadn't complained. They liked Clint and Ida around for company and also because they gave a welcome hand. Ida helped Sallie with the poultry yard, cooking and cleaning, and tending the young'uns. When he wasn't vetting, Clint pitched in with the farm chores, like helping his brother and Sallie get cattle in the cattle truck. Sallie would stand in the truck pulling, and he and Joe-Pratt would put their shoulders to the cow and push. This often made a hilarious, if nasty, scene, pushing a cow's rear end. If an accident happened, the two brothers would just look at one another and one would say the usual countryman's expletive, and the other would answer, "You better believe it. Lots of it too." And they'd laugh. "But it's just used grass," Sallie would add.

Joe-Pratt took pride in being a real farmer and not an ag-industrialist. He had row crops and a summer and winter kitchen garden that came close to feeding the whole family all year. "With our climate, no excuse not to," he said to Clint, and Clint agreed. This summer, at Clint's suggestion, he'd tried to raise his vegetables without chemicals and so far was having success. Besides the usual vegetables, from heirloom tomatoes and squash to butterbeans and okra, he had wheat and grain fields, millet, peanuts, fifteen acres of cotton, soybeans, an acre of purple ripper peas, half acre of watermelons and cantaloupes, and an excellent orchard he'd inherited from their grandma and granddad.

This year he'd put in an extra half acre of four varieties of heirloom tomatoes, Cherokee Purple, Pink Girl, Sease, and Goose Creek. He was trying the last he'd gotten from a friend down the road, who was now making a living at growing seeds for the heirloom seed companies. The surplus crop after canning, Joe-Pratt sold on a street corner in Clay Bank. The boys loved to do that. They liked seeing their work exchanged for the little extras they might not get otherwise. "Getting them started early," Joe-Pratt said.

The century old scuppernong arbor was loaded every year with bunches of grapes now already almost the size of nickels. Joe-Pratt always made several gallons of wine, and Sallie made the best scuppernong jelly. Like the surplus vegetables, her golden jars went to sell in town. The children had picked buckets of blackberries in June and July for jelly and cobblers, and the surplus again had gone into the precious jars that rivaled the scuppernong in popularity in town in the fall. She had her steady customers. The farm had a well-stocked fishpond and Joe-Pratt even kept bees, a fairly new project. This past year was the first he'd had honey to sell. His apples and peaches were some of the best in the community. Sallie made peach preserves for the family with a few extra jars to sell. Town-folk fought over them. Her pear preserves nearly caused a riot one bright fall morning last year.

But his real strong suit was dairy cattle and beef. His cows had the reputation of producing some of the best milk in the county. They ranged outside and fed on grass and hay, not corn. Joe-Pratt let them in the pea-vines after picking and raised extra turnips to feed them. The turnips, particularly, made golden butter and rich cream. Sometimes in winter, they got a little cotton seed meal. The meal was ground from their own cotton seed and also made the cream extra sweet and thick. He called his animals "Happy Cows" and dubbed his dairy "Happy Cow Farm." He sold a modest amount of milk at places like Kildee's Store. As fine a farm as it was, the brothers knew that to keep it going they'd have to diversify. This is the main reason Clint became a vet. Two big families probably couldn't make it on the soil alone. And both brothers wanted to raise a passel of children. Joe-Pratt wanted at least one more boy, and Sallie and he had always hoped to have a little girl.

They already had a name picked out—Tissie—after Sallie's grandmother. God willing, there would be no skimping there. Hang expense and what some folks called inconvenience. The children were a credit to them in the eyes of the community. A wise neighbour declared, "And you can't fake kids."

Clint told Chauncey as he ate his sandwich that he and Ida figured it would be best if they started looking to go out on their own. Sallie was expecting again. Now with Ida pregnant as well, the house, big as it was, might be a little too full. They needed space of their own. That is, if they could find a place and make ends meet. Clint hated the uncertainty of it all, but had learned early that was just life. You couldn't plan or predict its every turn. You just had to roll with it.

He wondered how Chauncey felt about all this, what advice he might have.

It was a question, by coincidence, well-timed. The answer might be a solution to Chauncey's recent quandary too.

The old McMorries Place had just come up for sale. It consisted of fifty five acres and a farm house a century and a half old. "A great place to fill with young'uns," Chauncey said. "And I sure would like to know who my neighbour is." The McMorries Place bordered his.

"How's the soil?" Clint asked. It was the perfect first question.

"Very deep and good. Has been fallow for years. What pine timber was on it has been clear-cut, so good pasture might be reclaimed."

"How much they asking?"

"What's left of the family is selling it on their own. That's a blessing. It'll cut out the middle man. The brothers and sister live in Atlanta, Greenville, Anderson, and Washington state. There are four of them."

"They want 150,000 for the land. The house, as dilapidated and unlivable as they say it is, is free."

"But that house is sound," Chauncey continued. "Made out of heart pine. Built up on brick piers off of the ground. The chickens old Mrs. McMorries always had loose in the yard had never given a termite a chance. That's a good old house. I know it well, and I went over there the other day to make sure I wasn't remembering wrong. Needs repairs to the roof, a few boards to replace, and a coat of paint, but y'all are like me. If I know y'all, you don't need climate control and don't want to be sealed in with vinyl siding, storm windows and doors."

"That's a fact. No need for a private bath with every bathroom, like a hotel."

Indeed, Chauncey did know them well. He counted Clint his son, the son he and Hoyalene, Clint's oldest sister, wanted so bad but never had.

Being so engaged in work and his duties as a newly married man, Clint hadn't heard of the sale. And the best thing about it for both Chauncey and him was that the McMorries Place lay along the complete south boundary of Chauncey's land.

"Damn, if this ain't too good to be true!" Chauncey said to himself. He was now especially glad that his desires had always been simple and few. He'd been a saver ever since a lad. The simple life, and no going in debt was the key. "Sit on an apple crate til you can afford a chair," as Trig's folks had always said. Trig had gone further and declared: "And even then, make your own split oak chair." Chauncey knew how good Trig was at doing this. He'd learned a lot from his friend.

The cash purchase would about wipe out his savings, but he could at least buy the place out right. He asked Clint how much he could do.

Ida had gotten a small inheritance from her Grandma Alston, who'd died three years ago. She'd put it in CD's to draw interest at the bank. It amounted to a little over 40,000 dollars. Clint had paid off his college loans and was just even. Soon, there'd be baby expenses, but giving over his part of their pa's land to Joe-Pratt would mean Joe-Pratt would pay him his share. Joe-Pratt was a wise one, and had a relatively fat bank account. He was shrewd with his cattle and planting and never bought things he didn't have to have. He raised most everything his family needed and even did odd jobs on the side. He was handy with a paint brush and hammer and could fix just about anything, from well pumps to wiring. Most men in the community could, but then there were widows and the elderly who'd call and count on him. He hated charging them anything, but even in reduced fees, the money counted up.

And Sallie was his biggest asset. If there ever was a smart woman, smart in the way of being industrious and economical, she was. She made certain there were extra eggs and milk to sell, and the fall jelly profits were not inconsiderable. This past year, with the bumper crop of okra, she had pickled two hundred and fifty pint jars of their family heirloom variety. These had gone as a trial to a specialty shop in Columbia as "Certified South Carolina Grown," and owing to the success, the shop owner had asked for her jellies and Joe-Pratt's surplus honey next year. "Certified locally grown" had suddenly become the craze. Next year they had lined up market sales for their half acre of watermelons. They were growing the famous Bradford family seed, much in demand by those in-the-know for its unmatched sweetness.

"Don't spend a penny," Joe-Pratt would say, "If you can swap and barter for what you don't have. Always have something surplus in your truck to trade."

And this he usually did, even if it was only a cord of wood to take to town in the winter.

"Can't sell from an empty wagon," their pa would always say.

When Joe-Pratt and Clint had talked money matters shortly after Clint brought his wife home, Joe-Pratt had said he'd be able to front him 60,000 dollars cash as part of what Clint had coming to him for his part of their pa's land.

When Clint told Chauncey this, Chauncey knew the scheme would work.

"Bring Ida over tomorrow if she's up to it, and we'll look at the place. If she likes it, it's a done deal."

"Can't believe it," Clint said. It was almost too much to take in.

Clint got in his truck and went home with the news.

Chauncey had Val McMorries' number at his office in Atlanta. It was he who was handling the sale.

Chauncey went straight inside and called. McMorries was not at his desk, but his secretary gave him Chauncey's message, and shortly after six o'clock he called. Chauncey had just got in from milking his cow.

"No. The place hasn't sold," McMorries said. He knew Chauncey as a neighbour, and had fond childhood memories of Chauncey's mom and dad. He was sixty four years old and two of his three children had been educated and were successfully placed in jobs in San Francisco and London. He was glad somebody over that way had remained home, and just as glad that it wasn't he.

"Since your land is the neighbour, I think I can speak for the others that we'd like you to have it," he said.

McMorries was a courteous gentleman. Chauncey enjoyed their talk on the phone, though it was interrupted half a dozen times by incoming calls and McMorries would have to put Chauncey on hold.

It gave Chauncey time to think though, while McMorries was having to make decisions, some of which, no doubt, were serious enough.

Chauncey had heard how Kildee had got the price of the old Ben Sims Place down for Dana just this year. With the recent downturn in the economy, it was a buyer's market. He'd try Kildee's same ploy. It would likely work because no one wanted farms.

"150,000 for the land, is that right?" he asked.

"Yes, and you can get a bulldozer to make short work of the house. It can be pushed over into the ravine. What you want to do, Chauncey, plant pines?"

Chauncey told the truth. He didn't at the moment rightly know what he was going to do but thought that since it was the adjoining land he thought he better buy it and decide later.

"I understand that well," answered McMorries. "We had to move to Crystal Hill and gate our community so we'd not have undesirables next to us."

"Bulldoze the house you said?" He couldn't believe McMorries brought up what he'd intended to do himself as a bargaining chip.

"You better get rid of it," McMorries replied. "The County is charging us a king's ransom in property taxes. And they go up each year. Bulldoze the house, and its millage is computed as pure farm land."

McMorries continued before Chauncey could say anything, "How about we knock off 10,000 dollars for the price of the dozer and clearing the house off the land. You just handle the deal and not bother us. In fact, with that agreement, let's make it worth your while knocking off fifteen."

Chauncey didn't have to put his plan into play, and he was glad. He didn't like to haggle or be even a little dishonest in any deal, especially over such an important thing as a home place, whether the owners cared a whit or not. He himself cared, realizing fully all the sweat, sacrifice, struggle, and love that had gone into it in the past and over so many years. At 135,000, he knew he'd buy the land himself even if Ida wouldn't agree with Clint. The price was a little steep for such clear-cut acreage around there, but not too far out of line.

After being put on hold again, he had had time to think. "I'll take it," he said. "Reckon y'all will have y'all's lawyers send over a contract and do what's needed on that end."

"Right you are," McMorries said. "We'll use the law firm connected with our operation here. They'll contact you tomorrow. Nice doing business with you. To be honest, I'm glad to be rid of the place. There's something to do all the time. Call the pulpwood people. Pay the poison spraying bills. Thinning and setting out pines. Paying the taxes. And it's always me. The money from the sale is coming at a good time. My wife's birthday's coming up, and I want to buy her a new car. And my last daughter's started college in Athens. I'm tired of paying her rent, throwing money down a rat hole. We've decided to buy her a little house near campus and let her roommates pay rent to her. Then we'll have something to sell at a profit when she leaves. That's the cost effective way to educate a child these days when universities seem to increase their tuition and housing every semester."

"Good plan, Mr. Val. You've always been a smart one with money. You got to look at the bottom line. Glad to oblige. Goodbye." With a click the line to Atlanta went dead. And that was that. He may have spent the majority of his life's savings, put up for whatever disasters his old age might bring, but he was glad.

He sat awhile a bit stunned with the phone still in his hand. In neighbourhood affairs like this, and with the river at your back, even the uncertain man would stand and act decisively. It was as surely a matter of freedom and life and death as faced Daniel Morgan all those years ago. Few might understand, but Trig would.

"You don't own it, you don't control it," Chauncey said out loud. He'd done with this new idealist's way of seeing land as not ownable, not being the property of any man. Property was the bedrock on which all rested. That had been the way in Carolina from the Charter of 1663 onward, and John Locke, its author's, own wisdom. Chauncey knew the lessons of history.

He thought, *No telling what folks nowadays would do to that land. Just no knowing. They've already sprayed the clear-cut with gallons of poison to kill the young sweet gums and anything else that's struggling to grow that might be competition for pines. Getting ready to plant pines. It looks like a war zone, like those pictures of France in World War I. Flame throwers had nothing on their methods of destruction. Then pines, pines, and rows of more pines, in a country that had always naturally had hardwoods, only to be savaged again in time with more clear cutting. An endless cycle of destruction, until the boron wore out and the land could not even produce pines. That was certain to happen one day—as sure as death and taxes.*

A few years back, some of the poison sprayed to prepare for pines had drifted across onto his land and killed a thicket where wild blackberries grew. It was the place bob-whites and rabbits raised. He knew that thicket well, not to mention that was where he picked blackberries for his pies. The raw brown of dead leaves looked like the plants had been scorched with fire. It looked so like a wound, a raw gash on the land. Every time he saw it, he felt in turn sad and angry.

"What you expect? Absentee owners," he'd

say. "They never have to see the damage they do."

Chauncey wasn't a greedy man, but he wanted that land, or at least for some good person to have it. He didn't want any more dead, chemically toxic brown places around him. He remembered a saying Farmer Lyman had passed down to the men at the store: "Old farmers would always declare, 'I'm not greedy. I just want the land that's next to mine.'" Of course that entailed rippling outwards like circles from a stone thrown into a pool. Chauncey reckoned he'd joined their august company as he hung up the phone. It was really after all not a matter of ownership but stewardship.

As he sat there pleased with the outcome of his endeavors, he remembered one of his father's sayings about having everything going your way. Chauncey recalled his admonition well: "Remember, son, be careful when you're getting all you want, fattening hogs ain't in luck."

He turned to his favourite picture of his father on the wall. His dad was in his neatly starched and pressed staff sergeant's uniform and his mother was by him. They were seated on the low rock wall his dad had laid in the front yard of the farm house with his own hands, a wall still there today, made of the native stone from the fields.

His father was at home on a furlough from Wiesbaden, Germany, as the war was beginning to wind down. It was their wedding photo. His mother was in her wedding dress, not the usual white gowned and veiled affair but a rather stylish 1940's dress with a typical 40s hat. She was a good seamstress and had probably made it herself. The dress revealed her good figure and was short enough to show a length of beautiful legs crossed ladylike as she sat on the wall, her hands in her husband's. She was smiling with that radiant smile she was always noted for, even to the end, when cancer took her. His father looked tired, as he must have been, with the pressures of war and the long trek state-side. He'd have to report back the following week, no time for a real honeymoon.

Chauncey took in all the details of the photo. In the background was the old porch with its wooden swing, the eight wooden steps leading up. The house was in need of paint. The yard was swept clean of grass and was spread with a layer of white sand. Bedraggled flower plots were edged with fieldstone. The quartz in their makeup glistened. The magnolia to the side that now today was quite large was just over head high. Even in the black and white image, its glossy green leaves shone in the sun.

The photo made Chauncey a little blue, but he'd not allow thinking of the losses time brings to dampen his spirits today. He let his gaze rest on the image until the light from outside dimmed and the picture blurred as he sat in the grey.

Stirring himself at the sound of the tabby wanting in the screen door, he prepared and brought her accustomed bowl of cream. She purred, her little motor-boat running, and rubbed against the cuff of his pants.

"Mowdie," he said. "Life is short. Death is certain. That's all we can know." Mowdie made no sign she heard him, intent on lapping her cream.

Ten

CHAUNCEY COULDN'T WAIT to give Clint the news, but he knew he'd have to in order to let Ida have the chance to say how she felt without his pressure or bias to influence her. She'd come to think a lot of him.

So next day Chauncey called Clint and told the two of them and Ida to go over by themselves. Clint told Chauncey to meet them there, but he declined.

"If you don't mind, I'll let y'all have this time alone," Chauncey said. "Y'all don't need distractions from a third wheel."

"You know we'd appreciate your take on the matter," Clint said.

"There'll be plenty of time for that," he answered. "Right now, I want you and Ida to be frank with one another about all this." He saw the gravity of the matter that Clint, at his age, didn't quite comprehend.

Probably better he didn't. He's got the enthusiasm and innocence of the young, he thought as he pulled out of his drive. *I wonder how he'd face that falling down farm house if he were my age.*

He'd make sure he'd not be at home, even if they came to get him, which they probably would. Another motive for leaving was to go down to Trig's. He had to tell someone what he'd done. To be honest, he was happy as a child. Still, he wanted to run all this by his friend.

The drive this morning made Chauncey's chest swell. Along Dogwalla Road, he often heard the *bob-bob-white* that always spoke to his soul. The high rise of the last note epitomized in some way all that this land meant to him.

Yes, he's a gentleman, that bird, Chauncey thought, remembering that's what his father always said. He lived close to the ground, and Chauncey liked that too.

This morning he heard the staccato cluck of a mother bird. "Calling up her young," his father would say, and in truth that's what she was doing. As he'd walked to his truck, he'd been startled by the whirr and rise of a pair and big covey of young birds. It was an occurrence that always lifted his spirits, much like the birds going up.

Encountering them there on his land gave him peace of mind and reassured him. Old

Farmer Lyman would always say that when you got bob-whites on your land, you're doing things right on the farm. Others said that too, Trig among them. He'd learned that from his pa, Trig said.

So Chauncey knew already that he'd done the right thing. Whether or not Clint and Ida decided favourably or no. Well, what if his nest egg was gone? He'd trust he'd not need it. Maybe he could work on and take care of himself and just go out like a light bulb. He'd have to trust to the Lord. Maybe Hoyalene and her long painful bout with cancer had paid his debt of suffering for him. He knew he was rationalising and that wasn't the way it worked, but you couldn't live your life scared. That was no life at all.

He had his truck windows open. *Bob-bob-white. Bob-bob-white,* the crystal clarion calls came again as he drove along. He wondered how many people today had never heard it. All the rushing and noise to get things had robbed this sound from their ears. He wouldn't trade it for any gadget you could buy at one of those warehouses on wheels. And certainly not for electric hedge trimmers, leaf blowers, weed eaters, or rototillers.

Maybe he'd swapped his nest egg for clutches of bob-white eggs. He smiled at the thought. He hoped he had. There'd been worse exchanges of things of value for things that were not. Most everything today was. He agreed with Trig when he'd say that for every step forward, we take two steps backwards. Anybody who might look at him and ask "What in the world Chauncey do you need with more land?" could just buzz off. He knew what he was doing and that the river was at all their backs. He wasn't likely to get that question from folks at Kildee's Store.

People in the town of Clay Bank, though, were a different matter. Like their reaction when he'd say he wasn't going to cut trees but just let them grow. Sometimes they'd smile and shake their heads. He guessed what they said behind his back. But Chauncey had long ago quit trying to explain things to them. It would just wear a body out and get you nowhere. It was like having to learn a new language to be able to talk.

He'd heard that the bank teller, knowing that Clint was Chauncey's friend, had volunteered one day while he was making a transaction at First Federal, "People from around here aren't smart enough with their resources. Take your friend Chauncey. He was in just the other day and I told him if he'd have his trees thinned, he'd be able to deposit a lot more than the figure he did that day. Turn green into greenbacks. Your friend just smiled and quoted some poetry."

Chauncey had learned from Ada Johnson, a neighbour down the road who happened to be in line behind Clint that day, that Clint had answered him after a pause, "You think Mr. Doolittle is bad about trees. He's middle of the road moderate, compared to me." That ended the lesson in finances. Chauncey appreciated the way Clint had come to his defense, but considering who the bank teller was and the Chamber of Commerce values of the market town, he didn't much concern himself with the fact that people in Clay Bank might be talking about him and his impractical, strange ways.

He remembered quoting poetry that day all right, and knew that doing that by way of answer would be enough to cause even more comment. That's why he did it there in that temple of Mammon. To them, it would be like cussing in a cathedral.

He'd said with an ultra-serious look on his face: "Well, you know, as the bard says, he that steals my purse steals trash, but he that steals my name puts his foot in it."

He'd left without looking to see the expression on the teller's face. He really didn't care.

Today, he didn't exactly know how Trig would react to the news of his plans. He thought he did, but Trig was always surprising you with an original take. He'd soon find out.

As Chauncey's truck was turning into Trig's yard, there was his friend taking a whiz against a fence post. Trig had his back to him, but knew from the sound of the truck who'd come on a call. He gave a little wave over his shoulder with his free hand.

Chauncey turned off the engine and Trig came on up.

"Well Chaunts," he said.

"Well Trig," he got in return.

They sat on the porch in Trig's big homemade rocking chairs.

"Can't seem to get going full speed today," Trig said. "Worked so hard yesterday, my legs are sore. Stove up all over. I'm moving about as slow as a crippled mud turtle."

Yeah, Chauncey thought. *Only Trig would come up with a* crippled *turtle.*

When he gave his account of yesterday's commitment, Trig didn't say a word. Then he paused for a minute and stroked his chin. There was a two days' growth of copper-coloured beard. Everything was so quiet Chauncey could hear the sounds the bristles made under Trig's hand.

He looked at Chauncey and the slant of sun caught his blue eyes. "I'm proud of you, friend," he said. "Didn't always know you had it in you, but I might have reckoned you had."

Chauncey figured he knew what Trig meant. Trig was always shaking his head at Chauncey and saying how he was such a safe man. "You don't take many chances and want the world neat. Plan everything," he'd often say. Trig had learned the world wasn't that way, and after Hoyalene's death and all the plans they'd made, Chauncey had moved in Trig's direction.

Trig had more chores to do. He was behind and still walked slow. Chauncey followed, giving a hand when he could.

He hadn't yet mentioned that Clint and Ida might be involved in his plan. Even in his own mind, he kept the thought at bay, trying not to presume. He was doing this on his own. If they wanted in, it would be the delayed icing on the young couple's wedding cake. That would be ideal, but Chauncey'd learned that the ideal didn't always get translated from sky to earth. He'd come a long way in his fifty-nine years.

When he told Trig of the possibility, his friend was pleased, and even got excited at the news.

"Clint's a good'un," he said. "That boy knows which end of the stick to hold. And Ida's as pretty as a blackberry flower."

Chauncey had never thought to single out blackberry flowers for beauty as many times as he'd looked at them, but on his ride home, Trig's image kept coming back to his mind. He considered awhile. *Yes, Trig got it right. If you don't look right close, you'll miss them. When you do, they're perfect. And then give them time, there's the fruit.* Trig could see the fruit in the flower. That's what he'd come to expect of his friend.

On the other hand, for the sort of folks he didn't much like, Trig had an expression: "bred by a buzzard and hatched by the sun." Chauncey felt that about summed up the careless manners of people, the throwaway sort with nowhere for home and no people for kin. The people who'd bleed the land for a fat purse. That's the world Dana had had to deal with, and the wonder was that she hadn't been ruined beyond hope. Even in his exhilaration over his plan, his mind kept circling back to her.

Eleven

WHEN HE TURNED into his yard, Clint and Ida were rocking on the porch. Clint was smoothing down the hair of the beagle's head. Ida had the calico cat in her lap. That's something Chauncey himself had never been able to do. But Ida had always had a way with animals. How appropriate it was she was married to a vet.

It was now mid-afternoon. Chauncey was right in figuring they'd been over to the McMorries Place all morning. They'd sniffed around the old house and got in by a pantry door. It was dusty and smelled like an old house. It needed a lot of work, but the ceilings were high, the rooms were twenty by twenty, the hall that ran the length of the house wide and welcoming. When they walked upstairs, the staircase didn't creak or give. The stair rails were made of black walnut, no doubt cut off the place. "Hand rails polished by the seats of little boys' pants," Ida had said. All the owners had had enough good sense not to paint them. The eighteen pane windows had most of their original glass. When Ida looked down at the overgrown yard from the second floor bedroom, she said it was like looking through crystal, and she wasn't far from wrong. The waves in the glass came from being hand poured. Each room had a big brick hearth and a high mantel above. When the McMorries family left, the house was still being heated this way.

Chauncey resisted the impulse to ask what their verdict was. "Trig sends his hello," he said instead. "I been down to his farm."

"So that's where you were. We came over after you," Clint replied. "How's he doing?"

"Stove up from yesterday's heavy work milling boards to repair his barn, but ornery as ever. Tired as he was, he still wore me out following him in his chores. He told me to tell y'all to come down to see him some time. He reckons you're busy, but hopes things will soon settle down."

Settle down. Yes, that was the lead in.

Clint cut to the chase. "We want it," he said.

Chauncey looked at Ida to see what he could read.

"Oh, Mr. Chauncey, I felt it was already like home. There's just some places you get a strange feeling like you've been there before. And this was one. I didn't want to leave."

"And you say you think we have a chance with the McMorries children to buy the place?" Clint asked.

"You sure you think you want it?" Chauncey looked from one to the other and back again.

"Ida?" Clint asked, looking at her.

"We sure want it, Mr. Chauncey. "We need it and it needs us."

"You think we have a chance to get it?" Clint asked again.

"You already have."

His reply puzzled the couple for only a moment. Then they suddenly reckoned what he'd been up to since yesterday.

Ida put the cat off her lap and came over to Chauncey's chair. She leaned over and kissed his cheek. Nobody said anything.

Then it took only a few minutes to give the rough outline of how the deal was cinched. They'd talk about particulars later, and knew that all three in the next couple of days would probably have to be visiting banks. This they didn't discuss in any detail right now. Instead, they enjoyed the moment, of being centred together in a bond as old as civilised man.

They talked of small matters concerning the friends and neighbours. This went on for an hour or so. Then Ida was tiring, Clint could tell.

"Well, much obliged, Chaunts," he said as he helped her down the steps. He wasn't taking any chance with a fall.

He looked back at Chauncey over his shoulder and his face showed his feelings.

Ida paused a second to listen to the bob-white's staccato notes. "Calling up her young," she said. Chauncey smiled a broad smile. "Fruit in the flower," he said.

"Surely," Clint responded, not knowing exactly to what he'd agreed and why. He'd properly picked up on the way it was said.

After they'd left, Chauncey sat a good while thinking over what the three had done. When he was making an impact on the lives of others, he always tried to consider every angle. Today, it was like handling a silky ripe peach, turning it over deliberately in his hands, before a careful enjoying.

As he went about his chores, he figured he'd

done the right thing. Two more farmers in the world owning their own land. God likes farmers, he thought. He made us from soil and for the soil. He knew the name Adam itself meant "of the clay," and he figured its colour was red.

As he closed the chicken house door, he could hear the occasional muted cluck of a hen, readying for sleep. It was always a comforting sound and brought back memories of his mother, whose sphere was the poultry yard. Putting down the tin feed bucket, he felt certain that Clint and Ida would make good tillers of the garden. The pail made its hollow clang and echoed off the barn wall.

Walking toward the back steps that led to the kitchen, his mind followed Biblical paths. When the Israelites demanded of God a mighty king to protect them from invaders, their prophet warned them that this mighty king they desired would take their fields, vineyards and olive-yards, even the finest of them, and give them to his lowest servants. God had been their mighty king, but they desired what other nations had, so He gave it to them, and His giving was a dispossession and a hard lesson too.

Chauncey knew this sad history, and the

seriousness of it tempered his happiness. Had this not been the way of his own country? A meagre light was shining in the hall. He could see it past the kitchen door. He suddenly felt tired and looked forward to his simple meal.

Twelve

THE CALL CAME from McMorries' lawyer next day about four. He wanted to discuss how the papers were to be drawn up and to get the proper addresses he'd need.

Chauncey was going to put the legal work in the hands of a distant cousin, lawyer Henry Dominick. He was an old-fashioned fellow who had an office on the second floor of an old brick building in Clay Bank. You entered the long stair walkup from its separate entrance on the street. The creak of the stairs and the echo that it made off the walls as Chauncey climbed to do his little legal business always pleased him, as did the leisurely atmosphere of the office.

Dominick had the usual law books, but also a whole wall of history, poetry and fiction on dark walnut shelves. Chauncey looked forward to having this unexpected reason to visit him.

Chauncey gave the Atlanta lawyer Dominick's phone number and address. When he got off the line, he called Dominick's office to let him know what had transpired. Henry picked up the phone himself. After a few minutes to catch up on news, Chauncey filled him in. "Congratulations on your purchase, pal. We'll take care of the sale, the title search at the court house, and the deed. Don't worry about a thing. That's what you got us for."

Chauncey liked Dominick's un-lawyer-like way of streamlining everything. He'd been a JAG officer in the air force for a time and had learned an amount of efficiency. His wife owned a small book store in Columbia, the one Chauncey frequented when he had to make a trip to the city. She specialised in old and out of print books that were hard to find.

As he put the receiver down, he breathed a sigh of relief. He sat still for awhile, then went to his chair in the alcove. Instead of reading, he closed his eyes and soon fell into a doze.

His sleep refreshed him and he woke to see a red tailed hawk circling high up over the line of trees on the ridge. The hawk had his mate with him and they looked like they were intent upon some intricately patterned dance. Watching their circlings and weavings almost hypnotised him.

First the male bird would dip and then soar. The mate would clearly echo the pattern but in reverse. It was like watching some kind of child's dodge-ball game or some kind of complicated dance whose steps were not known to man. Chauncey lost track of time.

He took a book from his shelf, one of his Gaelic language volumes, opened it on his knee, but after a few minutes fell back to a doze.

As he slept, the motion of the birds' weave blurred with the images of the words on the page. Some of their first letters were printed large and decorated with interlaced golden designs of men and women, animals and men.

In his sleep, he saw the circling birds become the words. The hypnotic sounds of the strange syllables he was speaking in his dream echoed like some ancient rhyme of making. At times the Merlin of his dream bore his own features, Merlin's hair turned grey like his own, and features grown wrinkled with age. Merlin carried an octagonal cane made from green ash wood and decorated with carved symbols of nosed moons and stars and fish of strange and Pleistocene aspect, like one that a character carried in a favourite book Chauncey would read every other year or so—old Uncle Ather, who stood up for the old order, the ancient way, the orchard keeper himself, living in the orchard itself and doing battle with the violations from a new inhuman way of doing. Fierce warrior he, but no match for the power hungry elite of a totalitarian way. Chauncey felt kinship to the author of *The Orchard Keeper* and wished they could sit down and talk.

Merlin raised his carved cane and the birds directed their gyre over it. They came ever closer in circling and instead of widening made a dizzying tightened vortex that swooped down with them to a point. He lowered his cane to become a staff and folded his hands upon it.

The old man raised his head toward the birds and said some of those strange words. The pair rapidly ended their descent, and settled gently, touching together on the back of his folded hands. He looked like an ancient falconer with twin hooded birds, each the mirror of the other, facing with touching beaks.

The bronze man's torso was the very same silhouette of the statue Trig had asked Chauncey to take him to see. Sturdy old Daniel Morgan, with arm vertically extended, hand on his sword's scabbard, the buckskin fringe of his arm hanging perpendicularly down, the sword become cane.

When Chauncey woke from his doze, it had grown dark in the room behind him. The last rays of the sun touched the top of the great white oak that Chauncey always called the patriarch of the place. There were some robins in the tree tops, their red breasts to the sun, taking in its last warmth of the day. They'd roost there that night and turn so their breasts would be touched by the rising sun.

"Robin red-breasts," he said aloud. "A good name. Like bob-whites and jack-married-the-widders and whippoorwills." He'd liked to have been Adam, who, in the fresh morning glow of discovery, gave things their names. The top of the tree was now golden, "splendidly golden," he said aloud. But splendidly golden wasn't quite enough. He wasn't quite up to the task of properly describing what he saw. He'd need Trig to name what it was.

"Gee, better get that milking done," he said to Mowdie who'd come inside and sat looking intently at him. "Bossy will be kicking at the barn door. Her bag will be causing her discomfort."

He got up with care. Like Trig, his legs were stiff from his work two days ago. Chauncey had noticed for several years now that he didn't recuperate from physical labour as quickly as he used to. He suddenly and all at once seemed to feel the heavy weight of time.

Putting on his cap that hung on the rack of a twelve point buck by his back door, he told the calico to shoo. The cat was under his feet. He didn't need a fall. He'd never even thought of that before. Reckon for certain he was getting old.

The cat was waiting for her bowl of fresh cream and Chauncey was an hour later than usual.

She followed him to the cow stall and sat and watched as the steady spurt of milk made its music in the aluminum pail.

It wouldn't be long now, she knew. For the most part, you could count on this strange forked thing called a man, leastways this particular one.

Thirteen

CHAUNCEY SAT at his kitchen table looking at the plat of his land. It was yellowed by time and tattered at its edges. It showed that the boundary line between him and the McMorries farm had one big irregularity. Chauncey's father had always regretted the pie-shaped wedge that ate a chunk of fifteen acres into his land. Chauncey knew well the story of how that wedge got there. His father had heard it many times from his own grandpa.

It had happened because of Reconstruction taxes just after the war. Grandpa said that it was only by shrewdness, determination, good luck, and the grace of the Lord that they'd been able to keep any of their land. Chauncey's pa added that it also took a rifle in his Grandma Toddie Doolittle's hand. She'd seen three sons brought home corpses, had looked long in their still faces, and so it felt good to hold such a fire arm. Grandpa Doolittle had taught her how to use it for protection during the war and she was a good shot. “She used it too,” Grandpa said. Those were the days when if you came on a body in the river, you didn’t ask questions and let it float on down. It was so like the days of Morgan and Marion.

Chauncey sat leaning over the plat. How hard the struggle to keep this soil. He thought about the generations gone, the sacrifices and sweat, the doing without, the blood and toil, the love of the land that it must have required. The morning light dappled the yellowed page. It made the paper the colour of old lace. A minute circle the size of a pin head, and .45 E.15 to the white oak. A circle and .35W.8.5 to the post oak, .25 E.39.16 to the red oak. A circle and .31 E.23 to the Spanish oak, .49 w.3.21 to the poplar along the Old Charleston Road.

Chauncey knew that the old roads followed Indian trails, which in turn had followed the paths of deer, panther, and bear. The natives had been there for thousands of years and knew best where to go, upon what shoals to ford streams. The white men had followed these paths too and with their wagons cut thoroughfares. The wheels had eaten into the impressionable soil. The old abandoned road bed on this map was nearly twenty-five feet deep on some points of Chauncey's land. He often walked there thinking of those old times.

And there on the plat was his creek. It twisted and forked as neatly on the page as it did in life. It reminded him of the loops of his scuppernong vine. And there sat the little drawing of his old farm house tucked into its hill. It was surprisingly detailed, the chimneys at each end, the two-storied porch at the front facing due east.

He could look at such maps for hours. If he'd been a cartographer, he'd have loved his job. He always admired George Washington more for his surveyor's skills than why he's remembered. That and his skill as a farmer. It always impressed Chauncey that he was the one who gave the mule to agriculture. *Back when the land was land* he'd sometimes say.

Such a fine careful drawing of artistic penmanship! Someone had taken a lot of time with this page.

But that's the way they did things in those days. Things were made to last and be passed down. There was a pride in signing your name. *21 February 1783. Marmaduke Coate, Surveyor* it read. Chauncey would have rather had it than a Monet. Certainly much rather than a Jackson Pollack or an Andy Warhol.

The dapples of light that danced on the page came from the sun shining through the maples at his door. The breeze shook them, and every now and then detached a flurry of fire-coloured leaves. In the silence, they made tapping sounds at his window panes. Winter would be coming soon.

Chauncey looked up. Was someone there? He listened intently for a moment. Only the wind and the leaves. He turned his attention back to the page.

When Clint came over that afternoon, he and Chauncey used their math to figure that at the average of 2,450 dollars an acre, that wedge ought to cost about 38,000, and Chauncey said he'd like to buy it, "to set old wrongs right," as he put it. His pasture would no longer be interrupted and his farm animals would be much obliged.

They figured that the full purchase price of 135,000 for the fifty-five acres could then be made up of Chauncey's 38,000 and Ida and Clint's 97,000. Paying cash for the total amount, the couple would still have money in their bank account, and Chauncey's nest egg would still be a big enough egg. He'd pay all the fees of surveying and recording and lawyering as well. While he was at it, he wrote Clint a check for 5,000 dollars as a house warming gift. He knew Clint would need to make some repairs right away and he had a baby coming soon. Chauncey didn't see how young folks just starting out could make it nowadays. He felt for them.

After they legally owned the land, they would divide it this way. Chauncey would add fifteen acres to his farm and have him a new neighbour too, a real one worth more than dollars in a bank. It took less than twenty minutes for Chauncey to walk to the McMorries farmhouse door. He'd already timed it stepping at a leisurely pace. "Once we've cleaned up the briars and dragged off the fallen logs and branches," Clint said, "It'll take even less." "We'll be sure to keep it worn," Ida said.

Clint looked at her with proper appreciation for her comment. His eyes thanked her. He hoped the lane would be worn smooth by many passing feet. Clint said he couldn't wait to have Chauncey help teach his boys and girls. "Better than a library," he said.

Ida linked arms with her husband and he gave her a kiss. She blushed a little. "You have to forgive us. The honeymoon's not over," Clint said.

So these doings took mostly a week, and what with his chores, he'd not seen Dana much. When he called her with the news, knowing he'd be running around with busy work and not be able to stop by, she brought him his pie. She had him a big casserole too.

It was good to be home, she said. "Don't believe I've been so happy in years. It's where I'm supposed to be. See you in church Sunday," she said and was gone.

Fourteen

THAT SUNDAY Chauncey arrived at church, as he usually did, pretty much on time. Rather than parade down the aisle with everybody there, he'd always take a back pew. The Hendersons took up the bulk of four pews to the middle left of the sanctuary. That's where Dana usually sat.

He was clean shaven and had his tie on straight. He noticed the smell of his after-shave, a thing he rarely used. It had been a Christmas present from Dana. He never thought to buy colognes.

This Sunday he saw right off that she wasn't there in her accustomed seat. That's the first thing he looked for when he came from the narthex into the sanctuary. *Wonder if she's sick,* he thought. *Or had an emergency.* He hadn't had time to call her Friday or Saturday.

Then he saw her and she gave a little wave with the paper church fan held in her gloved hand. She was on the back pew. She had a cream-coloured old-fashioned rose pinned to her blue silk blouse.

He slipped in beside her. She made him room and smoothed her dress. His linen trousers brushed her leg.

When they sang the opening liturgy, they shared the same hymnal. Their voices added to the swell of the room. Chauncey's voice was passing fair, but Dana's was superb. She'd sung for the Charlotte Chorale for a few years and even had a little voice training as a diversion from her troubles when Greg left home. The choir director at church had already asked her to sing with them, but for now she'd declined.

"Better stay a bit on the side lines. I'm the new kid on the block," she said.

Dana was shrewd in that. She didn't want to come on like gangbusters, she'd told Lula Bess. She didn't know whose turf she might be treading on. There'd been troubles like that in the Charlotte Chorale. Bess had said, "Suit yourself, but nobody'd think you're pushing in by joining the choir."

Just the same, she hadn't. To tell the truth, she was so busy, choir practice would have taken up time that right now, she didn't have. She fully intended to, though, later on, that is, if they asked her again.

There hadn't been any question in either of their minds as to which of the many little churches in their area they'd go. They went to the one they'd known from childhood, and their parents before.

Of the larger denominations, the Methodists and the Baptists of Clay Bank County, Trig about summed up the difference between them. "You know Chaunts, the difference between the two is that the Methodists will speak to you in the liquor store." But that really hadn't mattered to him or Dana. They were doing what it felt natural to do, and kept the comfortable old patterns laid down for scores of years.

After the service, Chauncey ate Sunday dinner with Kildee and his family. Four of the children, their wives, husbands, and grandchildren were there. Dana as well.

Kildee sat at the head of the long table in the dining room. Bess had put Chauncey by Dana down at the far end. The youngest children sat in the kitchen at the children's table, as it was called. Nolee May sat with them to attend to their needs, teach manners, and keep any overabundant energy and rambunctiouness in check.

Kildee graced the food with his thanks for the daily bread and for the company of family and friends. The meal was Bess's usual Sunday best. She and her daughter Katherine had cooked most of it yesterday, so they'd not have to skimp the meal by going to church. Kat had her fiancé Bo Montgomery with her at the big table today. He already looked like a part of the Henderson household.

Chauncey watched him. He was attentive to Kat without being overly so. He could tell they were comfortable with each other and didn't have to put on airs. Their behavior said, "Take me as I am, or you'd better leave me alone." That was pretty much the way it was with most people around here. Chauncey judged that Kat had inherited her dad's "Live and let live motto." Bo seemed to have that attitude too.

As he sat there and took the scene in, Chauncey was aware that all over their community, families were assembling this way. The Blairs up at Joe-Pratt and Sallie's were pouring tea like Lula Bess here. He knew they were because Clint had invited him there to share the meal.

They were, as usual, having his brother Chris, Nolee May, and their children, his sister Clarsie, her husband Eppes, and their growing brood all over for dinner after church. Clarsie and Eppes lived in neighbouring Fairfield County, so this was one of the ways for the family to keep its close ties. Chauncey would have loved to be there but had declined because Bess had her reasons for wanting him here.

The Grahams and Griffins and Subers and Gilliams were putting out their fried chicken and baked hams. The Eppeses and Leitseys and Simses and Kellys were passing round the cheese pie, rice and cream gravy, the last of the crop of Epting snap beans from the garden and the first mess of turnip greens. Bo said that at that moment Grandpa Montgomery no doubt was saying "Hand me that cornbread. Can't have turnip greens without cornbread." Bo had seen Grandma Montgomery shelling a lap full of butter beans out on the porch yesterday, and she'd right now be intent on seeing that everybody ate some. She'd cooked it the way everybody liked it with a ham bone and fresh cream. Bo's father was probably, as usual, pouring his butterbeans full of the sweet pink juice from a fresh jar of watermelon rind preserves.

Bo told Chauncey, "We've had some hard times in our family over the years, but we've always ate well, and we never turned anybody hungry away from our door. Some people might have called us poor, but we'd never be *that* poor."

Kat added, "And that must have included dogs. Never seen so many strays taking up on a place. Hounds everywhere."

"Dogs got to eat too," Bo said. "You know Pa and Grandpa loves their dogs."

"And like you don't."

"Bo, I knew your great grandpa well," Kildee came in on the conversation. "My dad got two of his best beagles from him. He knew his dogs. And he was one fine man."

"Thank you, sir. Sometimes I think I didn't deserve him."

"But I heard he could be ornery," Bo picked up the thread.

"Ornery is not the word for it, but ornery in the good way," Kildee said.

"Reckon we all got that ornery streak," Kat joined in. "I got mine from Pa."

"And your ma," Kildee added, looking at Bess, who ignored him.

Dana watched the pair. She was happy for her friend. Lula Bess hadn't made a false start like she had. Her cousin was the centre of a universe and when needed she was the gravity that kept its parts from flying to flinders in all directions out into a chaos of dark.

Dana had experienced that dark, when no pin-prick of light relieved it.

It was only at this moment at the table that Dana realised how unhappy she'd been. The contrast almost overwhelmed. The realization struck like the full sun after a total eclipse.

She was quiet for the rest of the meal. Bess noticed her changed mood and so did Chauncey. He hoped he'd not said anything that she'd taken wrong. He ran over a quick catalogue of things in the conversation, but didn't remember anything that could have hurt that way.

"I've been so stupid," she told Chauncey later when they sat on the back steps alone.

"Don't be so hard on yourself. We all make mistakes," he said. "And have chapters we'd just as soon not see published." They were watching Kildee's grandchildren play a game of tag out under the old orchard trees. Even though it was getting late in the year, they were barefooted. Not *barefoot, barefooted.* Chauncey thought that the ***–ed*** made their feet sound more grounded.

Next to the big May apple, the great Hebe pear was golden with fruit. One of the children delighted in picking up an overripe one and throwing it at a brother, popping him with a loud mushy wet *smack* upside the head. This unleashed great, gleeful laughter and a full fledged war.

"Such a fool," she repeated.

They sat there quiet. Chauncey told her of a fellow in town named Daryll, whose children had become estranged from him and how it was the grand children who had brought happiness back into his life.

"Sometimes, that's the way it works nowadays," he said. "My friend concluded that the reason he had such a close relationship with the set of grandkids was that they both seemed to have a common enemy."

Dana knew where Chauncey was leading and smiled to show she appreciated his gesture.

Chauncey continued, "Daryll said the children wouldn't probably reconcile with him even after he was gone. He'd just been to the cemetery to put flowers on his ma and pa's graves. 'Reckon I'll never get such from them,' he'd declared."

Dana said she'd had a friend at the office who'd said much the same about her children. She'd commented that it would take putting an ATM on her gravestone to get them to come by.

Chauncey was glad Dana hadn't lost her sense of humour. It would stand her in good stead, and now that she was back home, it would become stronger.

She had a palm flat against the porch step to balance herself, and he covered it lightly with his own.

He laughed a little at her quip about the ATM, and she smiled again. On her cheek, Chauncey could detect the trace of a drying tear.

Fifteen

SOME THINGS couldn't be undone, and because of the passage of time, some other things now just couldn't happen. Time had a way of marking thresholds and boundaries. Dana saw time as a progression of open doors. If you didn't walk through them right away, they might slam closed. If you did pass through, you'd have your back to all you left behind. Your view was relentlessly forward. More doors waited at every turn, and then the next doors you'd walked through would be at your back. You could only turn your head over your shoulder and glance, but never turn round and recross the same threshold. These images came to her many a night in dream.

Or that had been the way she'd seen time until recently. Now she was slowly adjusting her view. It was hard to fathom this thing. She was too closely involved to have distance to see. But instead of the linear thing, she was seeing time circling, doubling, weaving, intertwisting in harmony. The sun and the moon, the dark and the light repeating each day, the beat of the pulse, the monthly waning and waxing of the moon, the intake and expulsion of breath, the cycle of seasons, following each other but folding, returning back again. Even the generations of a family repeating old rhythms.

Memory had the power to short-circuit chronology. "There are no plot stories in life," she'd learned to say. That's why she didn't read novels any more. They just weren't true in the way they handled the world. They betrayed life. To her they were like forcings from some overeager control freak who wanted to put neat boundaries and fixed parameters on all things. Life wasn't lived according to outline or template design. It was a loose, flowing thing, its patterns as unpredictable as that big river a piece down the road. You'd never know what the next hour had in store. You couldn't plan. She resisted this trying to tie life up into neat little packages like novels, like some wedding or Christmas or birthday present in shiny paper and ribbon to be put on the gift table or under a tree. That was a way becoming foreign to her. It had never been a way of the people she'd returned to live among.

No, life wasn't neat and tidy that way and she now had the wisdom to know that it wasn't arranged just for her. She was learning that you could try and insulate yourself from life's shocks all you wanted, try to build an office wall around it with machines and screens as safe, distancing things, or make walls of books or videos, CDs, or DVDs, like so many bricks, but the shocks would come. She'd reached the conclusion that they could be the intensity of earthquakes and tornadoes, unpredicted the year, even the minute before.

Chauncey knew that Dana carried a lot of baggage from her marriage and breakup with Greg, more, she said, than the AMTRAK porters in Columbia used to do. She'd told him that she saw the before and after of her life as the negative of a blurred photo. She couldn't quite yet make out the lines, and the lights and darks were all reversed. She was still confused.

He told her that if he were in her place, he'd not give up on her son. Maybe she should try to focus on what she did rather than didn't have. He'd had to learn that lesson too. It had taken many years to get this far, and he was still working on it. "Life can never be static." He said. "The only stasis is death, and even that's a part of a cycle." He felt that modern science with its linear progressive explanation and view of everything, even its concept of time, had betrayed.

Chauncey knew he'd have to give her time. Maybe one day her wounds would heal and she'd be ready to walk through a new door. She'd taken big steps in that direction already, as it seemed to him.

But for now, he loved her company and they became closer as the weeks passed. She still had her teary moments, but he was a patient man. That was another lesson time taught. He tried to be sympathetic rather than judge. They had their little tiffs and disagreements, but both agreed that instead of trying to figure out whose fault it was, they'd work on a solution to make things better. She'd inherited another opposite way from her life with Greg and it was hard to put it aside overnight.

Billy wasn't helping much either. The other day a phone conversation with him had left her in tears. Chauncey decided he'd one day have to have a man to man with him. Right now though, time. Time. And patience too.

Sixteen

WINTER WAS IN THE WIND now in earnest these early mornings, and Clint and Ida had gotten two rooms ready so they could move. "A bedroom and a kitchen, that's about all we need right off," Clint told Chauncey. "We only had a bedroom at Joe-Pratt's; and a lot of times it was filled with Joe-Pratt's kids. It's been much easier to live in place and work on a room at a time than drive in for a spare hour's work. And being on our own for the first time has been extra nice. No matter how much you love your brother, it's not the same as having your own home."

Chauncey said that even though he didn't have a brother, he expected he understood.

The roof was fixed now. Clint had paid a roofer in town, who'd used Clint and Clint's friends to help him. That way, he'd halved the cost. And Clint's vet business had picked up appreciably. Folks were learning he was around, and he had no competition there or from town. Even some townsfolk were now calling on him for their house pets. He could see that this would be a real demand in the future.

The old barn at the McMorries place had possibilities. He'd already cleaned it out. It still had a good roof. Only a few pieces of tin on the western side had to be tacked down. The wood on the western wall had also warped and rotted. He'd fix that in time. Trig had volunteered some wood planks he'd milled.

But he already used the front for his vet's office, and that's where the clients came. Ida had stenciled him a sign. He'd hung it up proudly. CLINT BLAIR VET it read. Now that Clint had land, he wanted to farm on the side. He had exactly the forty acres of the old forty acres and a mule. All he needed now was the mule. The stall in the back of the barn could house him. "Get a gaited one," Chauncey said.

Maybe his vet business could eventually become his secondary job. Clint felt more and more that a farmer was what he was born to be. He'd really already known that, but the circumstance of too little land to share with Joe-Pratt had made him shove that knowledge to the back of his brain. Joe-Pratt knew his brother's sacrifice in going to college and now was so pleased that things were sorting out this way. He and Sallie would help them all they could. Sallie was already making plans with Ida to team up in her "Certified Locally Grown" projects. Having someone as a partner had given Sallie a real boost. "These are exciting times," she said. Ida had contacted the two fine restaurants in Clay Bank. They had committed to buying certain of Joe-Pratt's summer vegetables and the herbs she and Sallie were getting started. There was no reason she and Clint couldn't expand the project onto their land. "Their land," what sweet words. Chauncey was interested in getting involved too. He already grew several heirloom bean, okra, black-eyed pea, and tomato varieties

Now that the possibility of farming opened before him, Clint had also talked to Trig about his feeling that this was what he was meant to do, and Trig had told him the story of Golding Tinsley and his son Tira Tiller. "All us Tinsleys knew from the start that tilling is us."

"Back in the old days of sailing, Great-Great-Grandpa had also said that the boat's tiller is how you guide, how you move the rudder to plough your way through the water and keep the course. The steady North Star and a steady hand on the tiller, most all you'd need. You could fill your craft with rice, cotton, or indigo or the soft hides of deer, pelts of beaver, and the warm skins of bear and move them along the tidal creeks and rivers until you got to the great masted ships that would then go over the sea. That's another meaning of the word. And both fit right together with me. Us Tinsleys' rudder in life is knowing right off, what we was born to be."

Trig knew that the old McMorries place was good land. "It ain't been planted to death," he said. "As for soil, it's the story of your people on the land. That history can be read as clearly as the pages of a book, and up until the McMorries young'uns scattered every which way, the story was a good one. Even now, except for some timbering, it's not too bad a tale. Most of the land's been out of cultivation for at least twenty years."

Hearing Trig talk, Clint had suddenly grasped the meaning of "soil being in good tilth." He'd bring the McMorries land back that way. Circling to reclaim and salvage was really more his style than blazing new trails or setting out on some path totally new. His adventuring ran a different way. He'd much rather bring something good back to life than to clear great virgin forest trees for a new field. Clint knew that in the great dividing line in the history of the continent between the Stickers and the Movers, he'd have been a Sticker. Trig, Kildee, and Chauncey would have been too, and, in fact, were.

Chauncey had already known that about Clint. One evening last week when he and Clint sat on Chauncey's porch and looked up at the heavy harvest moon, Chauncey had gone inside to his bookshelves and brought out a book he wanted to read a couple sentences from. After a little thumbing, he found them in an essay by one of his favourite poets: "The task of the civilised intelligence is perpetual salvage." Focusing your love on one well-loved place was adventure enough. Clint immediately grasped the wisdom of this.

Chauncey didn't care much for labels—in fact, refused to use them, but in this circumstance they both declared themselves conservatives, going back to the root of the word. They conserved and salvaged, and supported and aided others who did.

"But none of your so-called conservatives of the Beltway kind," he'd said.

"Beltway conservatives. What a joke," Trig had remarked to Clint just the other day. "Them boys don't have a clue. Conserving is tied to having land and putting back into it as much or more than you take out. Land is where it all starts and ends. Them boys own condos and time-share resorts in the Virgin Islands, if they own any land at all. When you don't have a bit of soil to grow a respectable tomater plant to grow you a tomater to make you a tomater sandwich in the summer, then you don't own land, and you don't understand what government is all about." Trig's political acumen never ceased to amaze Clint. Clint told Chauncey he wondered how Trig kept up so closely without a newspaper or TV.

"Maybe that's why," Chauncey volunteered. "Like his talent at blarney and playing the fiddle, that's probably another of his natural gifts from the old sod."

As they watched the moon head higher over the fields, the bright orange glow burned shadows on the land.

"In the city, city boys thought I was crazy

when I talked about moon shadows," Clint said. "Or of hunting coon and possum by the light of the hunter's moon."

"Like Beltway conservatives, I reckon," Chauncey added. "They don't have a clue."

"Guess instead of making fun of them for making fun of us, we ought to pity them for being culturally deprived, or diagnose them with Nature Deficit Disorder and find some kind of cure."

"Wouldn't be found in a pill or a doctor's office," Chauncey replied.

The two sat in silence for a long while. Just saying or doing nothing there in their solidarity was the most pleasurable experience either could at the moment conceive.

Then Clint was gone. Chauncey listened as his footsteps in the crisp new-fallen leaves grew fainter and then disappeared down the path in the direction of his and Ida's new home. He used the moon to direct his way.

After a little while, Chauncey picked up his King James from the porch window sill. By the light cast from the hall, he half read, half remembered King David's songs of praise and celebration. They fit his mood perfectly this clear moonlight bathed night.

"Clint and Ida's new home." He liked the sound of the words. He felt good about having acted to help this happen. It was a long choosing indeed, this culmination of a moment in time, and he had had a part in it. He sat thinking about anything coming to the present out of the past requiring an unbroken chain of many people choosing to stay and preserve rather than pick up and go. There had to be stickers, and collaborations and covenants of the most elemental kind.

A long choosing. He knew Hoyalene would have been proud of Clint and of him. The wisdom of her last words yoking him and her brother in time was now as clear as the night before him on his blue lawn. Beyond the circumstances forced on her, she had made her choices too. She was part of that long choosing, and the place he stewarded was all the more sacred for it.

He dozed, then awoke to the sparkle of hundreds of lightning bugs in the cool dark, relishing their last sweets before the coming cold. He went inside but left the hall's great double doors open to the world.

Seventeen

IN THEIR CONVERSATION last night, Chauncey made it clear that if Clint would one day make farming his primary pursuit, and needed more land, he could count on him to loan him the use of some. He had more acres than he could farm. And with every year he got older, he'd probably need less. He'd rejected the alternative. There'd be no hiring of migrant workers. He felt doing so was a stealing of sweat. Not that they weren't good and honest farm hands. They were some of the best, turned off their own land by an empire's industrial schemes. Empire had its tentacles that far and he felt implicated in the process even though he had no direct involvement in it. Still Chauncey would be no part of this sad story of farm people dispossessed and victimized once again.

Back when Clint told him that Ida was pregnant, he'd visited Lawyer Dominick in town. That day he drew up his will with Clint as the sole heir. To the land, that is. Other of his things were left to Trig and Kildee. Hoyalene's few things, he willed to her oldest brother Joe-Pratt. He left Clint all his books. He knew Clint would be the one most likely to put them to good use.

"You're being smart to get this legal work done," Henry advised his friend. "Never know what tomorrow will bring."

He'd not told Clint about the will though. Chauncey didn't want to make him feel he had an obligation to him. Not that it would have affected Clint much. He and Ida did what they did for Chauncey because they wanted to. That's the way real friends were around here. Nothing less. Nothing more. They'd have appreciated it as the great honour it was, but their affection in no way could be altered by things. They didn't see love as a matter of what you could get out of the loved one.

It was this same foundation that the couple had built their marriage on. They'd reached the time when the honeymoon was over and would soon embark on that difficult second year, but Chauncey could tell there were no signs at all that it would be difficult for them.

This morning after his chores, and feeling

a bit tired from his work, Chauncey sat in his chair in the alcove with a new book open on his lap. It was a gift from Clint and Ida—a new edition of an old collection of eye-witness narratives of the Revolution in their area. John Logan, *History of the Upper Country to the Close of the War, Volume II* its title page read. Clint had seen it in a local history section of a bookstore, and flipping through it, figured Chauncey would find it interesting. They both liked local history. Clint had given it to him after Sunday dinner with Kildee and Lula Bess several weeks ago, but he was just now finding time to take a real look.

Clint had marked a couple of pages with Post-It notes, and Chauncey now read these. They concerned none other than Golding Tinsley. Tinsley and those who knew Tinsley had been interviewed as old men. Lewis Miles had written Logan a letter in 1858: *I have heard Golding Tinsley talk a great deal about the war. He was at the Battle of Blackstock's, when a British officer was riding on a white horse in front of his men. One of Tinsley's commanders said to him. "Can't you throw that fellow?" Tinsley replied, "I can try." He took good aim at him, and the officer fell to rise no more. Tinsley was also at Musgrove's Mill. He said they killed many*

Tories as they fled across the river there, and shot them while in the act of crossing. After the survivors had got over, one fellow squatted down, turned up his naked buttocks at them. Tinsley's commander said, "Can't you turn that fellow over?" Tinsley replied, "I can try." He took good aim, shot, and turned him over. They carried him off. Tinsley was a valiant soldier at the Cowpens.

Chauncey knew these accounts were authentic, being recorded so close in time to the living flesh. But, for all their distance from the events, Trig's own tales of these times sounded just as immediate and right.

He'd never heard these specific anecdotes among the many Trig told. Chauncey knew he needed a little break from strenuous work, so he got straight up, cranked his truck, and drove over to the Tinsley place.

He found Trig bringing in an armload of wood.

They sat down on the porch in the morning sun and Chauncey read to his friend.

"Well, I'll swonny," was Trig's reaction to the passages, using his old dialect word for "swear." "So that old fellow mooned Granddaddy Golding."

"Right. At least that's what he must have told Lewis Miles, who passed the story on down to Logan a hundred and fifty years ago."

Trig sat awhile trying to envision the scene. After a pause, he declared, "Well, Chauncey, I reckon that's an upside down sight not intended for view."

"Guess you're right again."

"And so Grandaddy Golding shot him in the butt?"

"Appears so. If a man's bent over with his behind aimed square at you, that's probably about all the target you'd have."

"Well, Chaunts, I'd never heard that particular story about him before. Heard plenty of others, but not that one. Guess it warn't meant for polite company."

Trig thought for a moment, chewing on a wheat straw. "I've heard of a crack shot, and Granddaddy Golding was accounted one, but this gives a whole nuther meaning to the expression."

Chauncey was amused at his friend. He chuckled to himself and thought *nether* rather than Trig's *nuther*, but didn't say it. You could take word play just so far.

In the absence of screens, the curtains from Trig's windows were blowing outside from their casements. Chauncey could feel the cool air from the inside blown out with them. Trig foreswore screens at windows and doors. Like Kildee at the store, he wanted dogs and cats to come and go as they pleased. As for window screens, Trig always said he didn't want to breathe sifted air.

Chauncey left the book with him and drove back toward home. On his way, he mused on their friendship over these many years, a stream of little events and humourous scrapes and quiet little moments from which in a phrase, gesture, or the look from the corner of an eye, Chauncey could gauge the true mettle of his friend. He drove at a creep giving himself over to a rush of memories, relishing them, looking more at the rear view than in front of him, for as truth would tell, he'd been down that road so often he could probably drive it blindfolded. He aimed to swing up to say hello to Dana and see what she was up to. If she needed some help around the farm in something she couldn't manage, he'd lend a hand.

As he was about to turn the curve that would take Trig's farmhouse from sight, he saw in his rear view that his friend sat in the sunlight, still in his rocker as he'd left him, the book open on his knee and the white curtains moving outside through the windows behind him like familiar and comforting ghosts in some kind of ritual jig.

"Wish Clint and Ida could see that. They've sure given Trig pleasure."

As if to echo his feelings, the sun, coming out from a cloud, lit Trig's stubble field. He'd cut the wheat just yesterday with a sharp-whetted scythe, and it stood up in neat sheaves, like soldiers at attention, awaiting the threshing, winnowing, and grinding, the ritual rhyme of making that led to the daily bread.

Eighteen

IT WAS THE SECOND full moon Ida and Clint watched from their own porch. As was usual, the sound of peepers, tree frogs, and crickets were the only ones, those and the rhythmical creak of their rocking chairs.

Clint picked up the King James he had on his knee and used it in their evening devotional. It was a ritual they'd started soon after they got married. Clint had learned it from Chauncey. The quiet of their new place made it easier too. They had added morning prayer to the routine of their day. The Bible from which Clint read had belonged to his grandfather and had an inscription on the flyleaf in faded ink, *Zachariah Rogers McMorries Blair, at his Confirmation, from his Mother, 10 May 1894.*

Ida said she liked to take time to think on their blessings, and to be thankful for the gift of another morning, the gift of another day. Clint knew that because Chauncey had lived alone for so many years, his whole working day had become like a meditation. He'd begun the way he and Ida were doing and his meditations grew, so that for long patches of time, he lived in a kind of constant prayer. The couple liked that about their friend and hoped to pattern after him.

Off in the distance, the music of hounds on a chase came and went. Clint thought he could pick out the voices of Chauncey's beagle from among the pack of hounds.

A whippoorwill sang out from the scuppernong arbor. Clint knew that the vines were over a century old, maybe two, and made a good night perch from which the bird could issue its assaults on the insect population around the home. No doubt a long procession of generations of whippoorwills had done precisely the same.

"When things don't get so torn up and disrupted," Clint had told Chauncey. "Then this is possible and nature moves in her own smooth way."

"The blessings of peace," Chauncey had replied.

Last week, Clint spent a full afternoon pulling honeysuckle from the arbor and had it once again in tip-top shape. With Chauncey's help, he'd straightened the cedar posts that held up the scaffolding.

"A rare and bearing vine," Chauncey had said out of the blue. Tonight, the phrase echoed with Clint. The arbor was hung full of honey-coloured clusters. They resembled the poplar leaves that were beginning to fall. "Amber days," the old folks called this time of the year, when the trees had begun to turn.

Ida had already concluded that the whippoorwills would have to share the scuppernongs with her this year, for she was planning to follow Sallie's example and make jelly for sale.

A Jack-married-the-widow called from the fastness of the distant wood. Clint taught Ida how to tell its cry from the whippoorwill's. His father had taught it to him. He often thought about his dad when he heard the bird's call.

"The whippoorwill's last note ends high," he said, imitating the call. "The Jack-married-the-widder's last note ends low." They were in just the right part of the world at just the right time to have both birds at one time. A rare thing. No. Unique. It happened nowhere else on earth.

That was a marvel to them both. They sat in wonder at it.

The couple looked at the heavy moon.

"About as heavy as me," Ida said. "It's taking a lot of time to get up, like me again when I try to get out of a chair."

The first nights they were married, they'd lain in the light of the waxing moon, and then when it got full, they'd made love every night in its light. The old tale went that if you did this, you'd conceive. From the figuring of the time Ida was due, it must have proved true.

They spoke of that this evening. Clint reached over and took her hand. The full swell beneath her maternity dress seemed to him to be as round as the moon. He was eager for the child to be born and to get back to married folks' ways.

They sat in silence for a long time until Ida broke the spell. "My!" she said.

Clint knew from the look of surprise on her face, that the child had given a strong kick. "He must be feeling the pull of the moon," she said. "Come put your hand."

Clint placed his palm lightly on the flowered print and felt it stir. "It's a strong one," he said.

They hadn't done the tests to tell if the baby

was a boy or a girl. "We'll just be surprised," Ida had said. But they both wanted a boy. It was a practical thing. A boy could be a stronger hand on the farm to help Clint. It might be the edge to help them make a go of things. Except for that reason, they didn't really care. God willing, they expected to have more to come anyway.

In these past months, Clint and Ida had got the old farmhouse in good order. The little room off of their bedroom was freshly painted, papered with designs of barnyard animals, and made tidy and snug. Baby showers given by Ida's sisters and sisters-in-law had provided needed baby things from booties to blankets for the crib.

Chauncey contributed the crib itself and a high chair. They'd been the ones he used as a child. His mother had carefully put them away in the attic, hoping he'd be able to use them for a child of his own. Clint had given them a new coat of shiny white paint. He'd carefully edged around the big decal of a yellow duck on the crib's solid headboard. Now after so many years, Chauncey was glad the crib would be put to use, a dream he'd had to shove out of his mind. He thought how pleased his mother would be with the way his baby furniture was about to be used.

Clint had gotten the two tall chimneys at either end of the house in safe shape. Owing to his labour, there were functioning fireplaces in all the rooms, upstairs and down. Most of the openings were so big that if Ida bent over, she could walk inside. Clint had installed cast iron stoves in the nursery and on the hearth of his and Ida's bedroom. This was a saving, more efficient way to heat. Joe-Pratt observed, "This way the heat don't all go up the chimney. The chimney's draw is so strong, it can suck a kitten up." He added after a pause, "They built things right in them days."

The Alston connection had already stacked Clint a neat wall of split hickory and white oak. They knew how much the Blairs were doing to help and wanted to use this good chance to get to know the new in-laws. "Best way to learn somebody," Billy Alston said, "Is working with them." Joe-Pratt and Sallie had pitched right in and the families meshed in their chores.

Ida's sister told Clint that families and not individuals got married, and Clint had agreed. He liked the Alstons. His brother and Sallie liked them too. They were struggling farmers like the

Blairs, and knew what mettle it took. Sitting there on the porch this evening, Clint and Ida talked about how lucky they were in having their families and that they got along.

The moonlight was bright enough now for Ida to pick up her embroidery needle and hoop. She was finishing the baby's white christening gown. "Good thing about babies," she said. "One size fits all. Unisex too."

Ida thought ahead to the happy Sunday when the gown would be used. All her Alston kin would be there. So would Clint's. After church, they'd have a big Sunday dinner here at their own house for the first time.

She knew she shouldn't be too sure of things and make too many plans. She knew enough of the world to realise you couldn't always count on having everything go exactly your way. With that understanding behind her day dreaming, she kept her feet solidly on the ground, but still anticipated with joy. And this was a particular joy she'd never known. Things were rounding out for her like the swell of her belly and the circle of moon she kept watching on its slow rise over the trees.

Throughout these last months, her joy must

have shown. People wanted to be around her. She'd been the centre of attention everywhere she went. "Everybody's so kind," she told Clint. People wanted to help any way they could. Especially the men. Giving her a chair. Helping lift grocery bags. Opening a door. Carrying things. Doing any little thing they could. A little girl at Kildee's Store had even tried to give her her peppermint stick.

"If folks don't respect and care for a pregnant woman among them, they're pretty worthless," Clint had said. For him, he reckoned the people around here had measured up.

Ida just hoped the baby would be healthy. That's all she asked; and judging from the power of its kicks, she figured it would. The little one seemed to be eager to get out into the world, to take it on with spirit and gumption. With the world as it was, Clint figured it would need that spunk to get on.

Nineteen

EXACTLY A WEEK from that night on the porch, Ida went into labour. When the signals came, Clint picked up the obligatory pre-packed suitcase and drove her to Clay Bank County Memorial where in less than three hours, their baby was born. It came a few days past the doctor's due time. Like they'd hoped, it was a boy. There were no complications with mother or son. He weighed nearly sixteen pounds—a strapping big healthy boy. The doctor was letting them go home the next day.

"He's got good lungs," his father declared.

"Lots of getting up at night with these," a nurse patted his arm. "You've now got a human alarm clock that sets itself."

The day they came home, Chauncey was sitting in his truck in Clint's driveway waiting for them.

Clint had called him last night the time the baby had come. He'd been too busy before to let him know they'd gone. The hospital let Clint stay with Ida and the baby that night on a cot in their room, so he hadn't been home. Today he'd phoned Chauncey again to let him know they were on their way home.

Chauncey had time to think as he sat there in the truck. He thought back to his mother and the kindness she'd shown him as a child. That, and Hoyalene and the sorrow they'd felt at her miscarriage. He remembered how Hoyalene had made the choice to get pregnant again even when the doctor had said that it was risking her life. They'd not known about the cancer at the time. When she died, little Clint had grieved over his sister as much as Chauncey. Everybody worried about the lad. He'd go off into the barn to be alone for long hours at a time. It was that which was the bond that brought Clint and Chauncey together from the start, that and the fact that Hoyalene and Clint bore the same blood. As Clint grew up, Chauncey could see they resembled one another in so many ways.

The day Hoyalene lay beneath the tubes and struggled for the breath to tell Chauncey to take care of Clint, was as close to him as yesterday. He remembered every detail of the room, every pause between her words, the look of her pale face, the gauntness of her cheeks, the tenderness in her eyes through her pain.

Before he'd left home to come over to Clint's, he'd taken Hoyalene's gold locket from his dresser and put it in his shirt pocket. Now, he took it out and held it in his hand. His eyes followed the interlacings of the engraver's swirling design on its case. After awhile, he mustered the courage to snap the locket open and look at the two images. There was Hoyalene, as bright as ever, eyes shining, the light on her black curls. That broad smile like sunshine. It still took his breath. And he, his image in its compartment facing hers, her favourite picture of him. Collar open. A new-tilled field behind, and just discernable, a couple of beagles romping beyond the path where he stood. It was made on the day of their first anniversary. He looked so happy there. It was a blessing not knowing what was in store.

Chauncey's reverie was broken by a gust of wind that sent leaves peppering against the truck window. Then in the distance, he heard the sound of Clint's truck turning in the lane. He looked up to acknowledge a fair lovely day, almost seeing it for the first time. As he waited for the truck to come into view, he noted how

Clint's good work on the land already showed. Chauncey was pleased with how much Clint and Ida had done in so short a time. True, they'd had help from Alstons and Blairs and a number of folks, including himself, but much of the work was their own. Everyone around already knew that laziness was not part of their makeup.

When Clint's truck came in sight, Ida was holding the little one up to the window and moved his hand in a wave. It was like the minister holding up a newly christened babe to the congregation, walking down the aisle from the baptismal font, presenting it to its new church family.

Clint helped Ida out of the car, and Chauncey assisted him in bringing in their things. They got all the necessaries in to the nursery.

When they finally had a moment to pause and look at one another, Chauncey spoke.

"Well Clint," he said.

"Well Chauncey," Clint replied with a broad bright smile that always reminded him of Hoyalene.

"Come hold the baby," Clint said. "Little Chauncey Blair." Ida handed him the child.

Chauncey really didn't know how to hold a

baby. Putting him on the spot to figure it out didn't let his mind relish what he'd just heard. Ida showed him how to support little Chauncey's head with his hand.

"Guess you're gonna have to get use to this," Ida told him. The baby, who'd been asleep off and on through most of the trip, slept soundly again.

Chauncey now had him cradled in his arms. "Little Chauncey Blair," he said softly. He repeated the name in his mind, as if to verify that he'd heard it right and to let the reality that they'd done this for him sink in.

They'd surprised him with this. Clint had kept the secret well. The couple had planned all along that if it was a boy, they'd name him Chauncey, and that at the christening, they'd ask Chauncey to stand with them and accept the little boy as his god-son. Chauncey still hadn't heard this last, so there was yet another happy surprise in store.

"Little Chaunts," he repeated. He didn't quite know what else to say. The three grownups and the newest member of their world were all silent for a space.

Better not handle this with words. Chauncey

kept his peace. For Ida and Clint, Chauncey's look was all that was needed to say.

Around these parts, actions meant more than words anyway, and words only counted when actions accompanied them. "A shape to fill a lack," Chauncey would sometimes call the word in isolation from the deed.

When Little Chauncey was comfortable in his new crib and he and Ida stood over him alone, Chauncey took Hoyalene's gold locket out of his shirt pocket and placed it in her hand, closing her fingers gently over it. She knew from Clint, how, until recently, he'd worn it everywhere since she died, never taking it off.

"For Little Chauncey, his Aunt Hoyalene's, when he gets old enough to know," he said.

Then it was Ida's turn. "Well Chauncey," she said.

"Well Ida," he replied. And once again it wasn't words that told the tale.

Twenty

WHEN MR. SUDIE EPPES had his fall and got bed-ridden from a broken hip, he couldn't take proper care of Bernie T. any more. So Sudie gave him to Trig. Trig already had hounds a-plenty, but Bernie T. was special, and he wanted to do Sudie a favour too.

"Trig, you're always trying to do too much. I know fodder-pulling time is a busy season of the year, but you need to slow down a little, and fish my pond," Sudie told him. "And that'll give Bernie T. the chance to do what he's famous for. It's a talent I'd hate see go to waste now I'm put to fallow."

Bernie T. was what Sudie called a fishing dog. And Trig had witnessed him more than one time at work. He was the only such dog in existence, far as either of them knew.

He didn't jump in the water and catch fish with his teeth or pounce on them with his paws. No. He did even better. He caught fish without getting wet or ever even leaving the bank.

Bernie T. was a Heinz-57. In his breed, terrier was probably the dominant strain, but you could squint your eyes and see beagle and a little setter too. There might even have been a little Boykin Spaniel thrown in.

One ear stood up and one ear flopped down. He looked the equivalent of the scrappy city kid who took to basketball and baseball and all games easily and was street wise. His energy was boundless. He never missed a thing. Around these parts, he was called a fyce or feist, a name given to any yappy, scrappy little dog with spunk and heart.

"Too much heart," Sudie would sometimes say of him.

Sudie hated to part with the dog, but his wife Sadie had too much on her hands already. Taking care of Sudie was enough. She didn't need another mouth to feed. And she wasn't feeling too spry herself.

"When I hit seventy," she told Trig, "I felt like I was a day older than water and two days older than dirt." Putting Sudie in a nursing home was out of the question, as long as she could hold up. Sudie had one main wish now, and that was to die at home. Sadie figured that wasn't too much to ask of the world. She reckoned that to Sudie a nursing home would be like a sentence of death. "But for a crime he ain't committed," she told Trig.

So Trig lessened their load and took Bernie T. It was the least he could do to help out Sudie and Sadie. Besides, he loved fish and fishing too. It was the best relaxation he could ever imagine, especially when you had Bernie along as your companion at the pond.

Today Trig was happy as a lark. He'd strode down the lane through cows and horses and arrived at Sudie's pond in early afternoon. It was a perfect late fall day. Only the soreness in his legs kept him from feeling perfect too.

He'd worked hard all week, and this Saturday excursion was his reward. He had two cane poles over his shoulder and a rusty gallon paint can full of worms. He'd gathered them from a big pile of last fall's rotted leaves that he was folding into his compost heap. Finding the worms as he was performing the task two days ago had in fact given him the idea to come today, that and watching Bernie T. seem to pine away with inactivity.

"Would be a shame to waste these fat worms,"

he'd said to Bernie. "And waste the world's only fishing dog."

Slung over his shoulder, he had a rolled up camping mattress. It was a fancy one with the *Wild River Outfitters* label still on it. The mattress had blown off a camper trailer driven by city folks who came to canoe down the Tyger— "the last real wilderness experience left in the state," so the trail guidebook proclaimed. Trig figured the driver was rushing to his destination so fast that he probably didn't notice when it flew off. After a day, when nobody had come back for it, Trig appropriated it from the Queen Anne's lace and goldenrod on the side of the road. As for the guidebook's wilderness, it was just home.

He was fishing for bream. Sudie's well-managed pond was full of them, some bigger across than your hand. On the odd chance, he'd sometimes catch a bass.

Trig wasn't one of the catch-and-release sort. He loved to eat fish. He liked to fry them up outside in his big iron pot, and especially this time of the year, when the days had shortened down cool, but were still long enough to give you daylight to do the frying for supper.

Cool weather brought an appetite for a lot of

fish that hot weather never really did. Trig liked to leave the tails and fins on. He fried them up crisp so the tails would crunch when you bit into them. He had the reputation of being an expert at a fish-fry, something he'd learned from his grandpa.

It's all in the heat of the grease, Grandpa Tinsley would say. Pop'em in the fat, and when they float up to the top, they're ready to eat.

If he caught enough, he thought he'd invite Chauncey and Dana over to share.

Bernie T. was at his heels, or to be more accurate, was darting ahead, cured from his doldrums, and taking everything in. He'd been taught better than to fool with the cows and horses, but everything else was fair game. He chased a fat brown grasshopper that flew and stopped and flew again. The ideal little dog tease.

His pair of poles thrown out into the pond, Trig settled down. He put field rocks at the base of his canes in case of a breeze. He unrolled his camping mattress and placed one end up against a stump for a pillow, and there he reclined.

He exhaled a sigh of relief as he eased down on his elbows.

The sun, for late September, still had strength. Trig lazed in it, and soon fell into a doze.

He'd just been telling Chauncey last week how he couldn't recuperate from strenuous work like he once was able to do. Not too long ago, a good night's rest and he'd be ready to go at it once again early the next morn.

"Now it takes two days," he told Chauncey. "And on the first, I just ache and turn stiff as a board. Feel like I've been run over by a truck."

"Know what you mean." Chauncey replied. "Sometimes it takes me three." Chauncey added that he'd just said the same thing the other day.

In another year, Trig would have his sixtieth birthday, and this coming milestone was already causing him to reflect. Seeing Sudie bedridden and giving away special dogs had also caused him to think. And Sudie was just a little more than ten years older than he was.

So Bernie T. was the perfect fishing dog. Trig could sleep and catch him a mess of fish too—both at the same time. He wouldn't have to aggravate the aches in his hips and legs. He could rest after pulling fodder yesterday.

There sat Bernie T. next to him on his haunches, his face fixed straight ahead at the glassy smooth surface of the pond. He didn't move a bit. His eyes were trained on the two red and white corks. He sat at attention, like a soldier dog, like those animals from dog college you could say *Stay* to and they'd stay.

The fish weren't biting yet for whatever reason fish had, and soon Trig was sound asleep. After a while, he was snoring there in the sun. Bernie T. kept his fixed gaze.

A cow ambled down out of the high field. She came to investigate. She walked within a foot of Trig, but still he snored. She sniffed at his arm and wrapped her tongue around a bunch of small white daisies at his side. She gathered them in and chewed. A green drool fell close to Trig's sleeve.

Such a racket of snoring! It may have scared the fish away. Bossy, her curiosity satisfied, moved on to the pond's edge for a drink.

Through all of this, Bernie T. hadn't even looked her way.

Bossy went on back up the hill.

Bernie still sat at attention with his fixed gaze.

Trig still snored. He mumbled something in his sleep, slapped his face for a fly or mosquito that bothered him. Mosquitoes were still out.

There hadn't been a freeze.

Not a cloud in the sky. Not a breeze. But for Trig's snoring and with the cow gone, all was quiet and perfectly still. Not even a ripple on the pond.

Its silver smooth water looked like polished steel. The world seemed in a trance, some mystic mood when time and reality melted away leaving only the white autumn glare of the sun.

Bernie T.'s eyes were even more intently now fixed straight ahead. It was the supreme stare of meditation. His white coat sometimes trembled a little with anticipation. It was like a shiver ran over him every now and then.

All this inaction was performed to the hypnotic rhythm of the intake and expulsion of Trig's breath. His snores had ceased and he was sleeping peacefully, his head cradled on his arm like a bird drowsing with its head tucked under its wing.

Was it illusion? Or did that first cork bob? No mistaking. It bobbed again. The second dibbled too. Trig was getting a bite, maybe two at the same time.

The racket of Bernie's barking shattered the

frozen air and they were back in time. It was as startling as stepping on a sheet of skim ice on the pond. The corks now danced. Bernie's racket got frantic. The corks were moving out toward the middle of the pond. Soon the canes would be pulled too. If Bernie T. could have cut cartwheels, he would. Instead he tugged at Trig's sleeve.

Trig knew the drill. First one. Then two. He had two bouncing, splattering bream. The sight of their golden scales in the sun was a pure delight, both to Bernie T. and Trig.

Trig laced them on his stringer, re-baited his hooks and put out his poles again. The fish on the stringer swam around in circles. No more freedom for them.

Bernie T. had reached nirvana once again. His gaze negated time.

After slapping at a few mosquitoes, Trig had gone back to sleep. He turned his shoulder more deeply into the mattress propped with its head against the stump for a pillow.

A water snake swam toward them, reached the bank, and lay outstretched still in the sun. It had its plenty of minnows and frogs and was now full and satisfied. The bumps of its prey showed on its sleek body like the links of a chain or beads on a string. Its scales shone like a new penny. Soon it would be looking to hibernate. But for now it lay motionless in the sun.

Bob! Dibble. Bob! The racket again and tug at the sleeve.

The snake plopped off the bank on its belly and was gone. Its ***S*** movements in the water hardly left a wake.

Trig strung another bright fish on the cord. The first two bream now swam less vigorously. The new one carried the others along, not having the wisdom of the earlier two. "No need to fight it," the pair seemed to say.

"Yes, this getting old takes some getting use to," Chauncey had told Trig. "Another month I'll turn sixty."

At that, the two friends had sat silent awhile. They were at Kildee's Store, and Kildee had overheard.

Kildee would soon turn sixty-four. His wife and Chauncey were the same age.

"I told Bess the other day," Kildee said. "That with every year since sixty, it seems like I age ten. Whenever I get up in the morning, I got aches in places I didn't even know I had. But for all that, the year passes just like a day."

"Remember how when you were eight or nine, a year seemed like it would never end?" Chauncey asked. "How the next birthday to come seemed like it would never get here? How waiting for Christmas felt like an eternity?"

"Yep," Kildee reflected. "How when you're six, you'd correct and say 'six and a half,' when somebody asked your age, taking real offense at just six."

"I reckon when you're six, a year is one sixth of your sum total of life, and for that reason seems like such a long time," Trig said. "But at age sixty, a year's just one-sixtieth and feels like a tiny dot in the big scale of things."

"Hardly a blip on the radar screen," Chauncey agreed.

"All the blips seem like they're in my brain," Kildee replied. "I keep on forgetting things. I'm getting bad. Bess thinks I'm getting old-timer's disease."

There on the bank, Trig thought about their discussion at the store last week. In between sleep, pulling bream from the pond, and baiting the hooks for more.

The mosquitoes had gotten more numerous

with the late afternoon. This year with the bountiful rain, there had been more than the usual. Trig in fact had told Kildee that the mosquitoes around here had so much of his blood that they were nearly kin.

He now had twenty good size bream, a small largemouth bass, half a dozen respectable ones, and he'd had to throw back only a few.

Bernie T. and he were a good team—Bernie T. the perfect fishing dog, the only one of his kind.

"I reckon I better slow down a little like Mr. Sudie says." He looked over at Bernie T. But Bernie paid no attention. You guessed it. He was looking at corks.

The sun was dropping low in the sky and there was a chill in the air. The water had turned the colour of khaki but was still smooth as glass. Trig was thinking about the mystery of it. So calm on the surface but deep down there, everything was just eating the hell out of everything else.

"Better be getting on back." But he left the poles in the water as he took his time in rolling up his mattress and gathering up his things.

"Always room on my stringer for one more fat bream." He watched the electric tremor of anticipation run over the dog's hide.

"Till I get home, it'll be past bull-bat time. I got to milk and there's all these fish to clean."

Bernie T. looked disappointed and whimpered as Trig pulled in the poles and wrapped their lines. But he followed dutifully as his master made his way up the lane that led from the pond.

The fish in the tin bucket gave an occasional splash as Trig crested the hill. They seemed to know they were being taken further and further from home, some kind of forced march they'd never envisioned before, and from which there was no return.

Now the bottom rim of the great orange disc just touched the dark tree line. The first bull-bat flew overhead, dipping and circling frantically, in pursuit of a meal. It was soon followed by a second and third.

Trig quickened his pace. The sight of them always signaled milking time. He was glad he didn't have a long walk home. Time had stood still for a while but now he was back in its flow.

A gust of wind detached a cluster of leaves from a tall oak, and one grazed Trig's ear, another his cheek.

"Soon be another year," he said to Bernie T. "Leaf kisses is the only ones I'll get, excepting it's a lick on the cheek from you." Bernie T. trotted up close to his heels.

The gust had a hint of winter in it, and Trig rested his poles and bucket for a moment while he buttoned the top button of his shirt and zipped his jacket up.

They were well on their way now. They'd make it back home in time. The cow would be waiting, and probably out of patience, maybe even kicking at the planks of her stall.

"Everybody says slow down," Trig looked at Bernie T. "Great advice, but I wonder how. Time don't stop for a rest. For you, I reckon, it's just a cork that bobs. But me, I got to carry the poles. Only way I'll be able to stop is when time knocks the pins out from under me and lays me in the ground."

Trig could have sworn from the look of him that Bernie T. understood. He cocked his head so that the one raised ear pointed at Trig, and as if to say that he was in total agreement and they were perfect friends. They worked like clockwork, hand and glove.

Twenty-One

CHAUNCEY HADN'T BEEN the twelve miles to Pat's Place in several months. But today he had a hankering for barbecue, and Pat made the best. The sauce was just as Chauncey liked it, being brought up on the local mustard-based blend.

Patrick Graham was almost as good a reason to go as the barbecue. He was six foot five, weighed 250 hard pounds, and had the deepest voice Chauncey had ever heard. He was a man of few words, but when he used them, they counted. He could tell some good tales if you could get him to.

Pat ran the place with his wife, two married daughters, a son-in-law, and two sons, one in his teens. The other was his oldest boy, Chad, who'd just turned twenty-six and was his chief cook. Chad's wife could be counted on to waitress in a pinch. Chad had the reputation of being able to deep-fry anything to perfection. As he told folks who asked how he did it, he said that the secret was to get the grease hot, and in order to do so, he didn't mind risking burning the place down. The last may have been an exaggeration, but was at least half serious.

Pat farmed on the side and opened the restaurant only from Thursday to Saturday. "Got to do more than farm these days," he'd say. "I draw the line on Sunday though. That's the Lord's day." Old Reverend Drafts had said that it was alright to work on a Sunday if the ox was in the ditch, but so far the ox wasn't in the ditch. Pat was able to provide.

The reason Pat's barbecue was so good is that he put the hog on the pit the day before and his boys slow-cooked it all night with hickory wood. The sons raised the hogs on restaurant left-overs and natural forage. That was another major reason the meat was so good.

The restaurant sat on a country thoroughfare called New Hope Road. As Chauncey drove there, he thought that maybe the name was an omen. He wasn't sure though. He wasn't exactly an optimistic man, but he did have hope. A few years back, Kildee had explained his take on the difference. "Well, Chauncey, like you, I'm not optimistic about the future, but I do have hope. Optimism smacks too much of a big program, and you know how I feel about big programs. We've had too much and too many of them. They got us behind instead of ahead. But hope is a Christian virtue though, and I don't argue with that."

On his drive, Chauncey noted that the Clay Bank County road crew had been at it again. The cedars grown up on the fence lines or bordering the woods had been sheared savagely. The county had bought an expensive new green shearing machine—all teeth and noise—whirling blades at the end of an arm that could project thirty feet in the air. Chauncey guessed that it was another new plaything for the McWorld in love with machines.

"What a waste," Chauncey had said when he encountered it the first time. "One day we'll regret spending that money and need it back for necessities." He had a devil of a time keeping the machine off his road frontage, but there in the middle of the asphalt, he made his stand and won. His grandpa hadn't signed over the right of way back in 1949 when the road was paved, so the county had no legal claim. The supervisor had his big Doomsday book, its pages listing each person who'd signed and each person who hadn't, ready with him in the front seat of his truck, and when he looked up the location, he had to admit that Chauncey was right. Grandpa Doolittle hadn't signed. As Chauncey knew from his father's accounts, he hadn't wanted the road paved through their place any way. He didn't have a car and suspected anyone who did. The only people who needed them, he said, were doctors, lawyers, and fools. Knowing his grandpa's reputation as a curmudgeon, still legend a half century later, his surmise about not granting right away had saved Chauncey's trees, and on that day of the showdown with the supervisor, Chauncey, silently and sincerely, gave his grandpa proper thanks. Like so many of his people who'd lived there on the land, Grandpa was still giving to him in small ways and big. Chauncey knew how many had collaborated to provide him the stable foundation on which to stand and survive. He was so lucky in that, the gift of real sustainability, quite a buzz-word these days.

Along New Hope Road, the trees hadn't been so lucky as at Chauncey's. All the cedars and other shrubs unfortunate enough to catch the road crew's attention looked like they'd been sliced through the middle by a buzz saw. On the fence lines, they'd been cut off at five or six feet and had a strange decapitated look. The mutilations on any other day would have put Chauncey in a foul mood, but today he let it slide. He tried not to see the brown patches of dead vegetation along the road sprayed with chemical poisons.

The restaurant sat square in the middle of a twenty-five acre cotton field that belonged to one of Pat's brothers. It was surrounded by woods. These were Pat's. They provided the logs for the pit. One of the sons-in-law cut and stacked it for him in the lean-to shed out back by the cooker pit. This afternoon the cotton was white with fully-opened bolls as far as the eye could see.

Blue Bessie fit in well enough with the trucks in the gravel lot, but it was by many years the oldest one there. A couple of the vehicles were giant expensive things, with lots of chrome, big cabs, and a high-polished shine that hurt your eyes in the September sun. To Chauncey, they looked like tanks. The truck next to him had stickers in the window reading *Pure Rebel* and *Eat Beef. The West Wasn't Won On Salad*. Another's bumper read *Go Ahead and Honk. — I'm Reloading*. Chauncey agreed that it was ill-mannered to blow your horn trying to get someone to speed up. Folks didn't do that around here, but folks from cities often did. He felt certain that a few seconds lost in the service of courtesy was more than an even swap. He liked the spirit of the decal.

He passed a truck on the way to the porch that had a Christ fish emblem and a slogan saying *The Body Doesn't Have a Soul. The Soul Has a Body.*

Chauncey noticed all these little things. As an only child and a man who had seemed to live most of his life on the edge of some great profundity, he was a good, patient observer, waiting, and paying attention to details. He'd gotten in the habit of looking at the world from the margins. Poets did that too—leastways, as he felt, the good ones did.

Chauncey came by himself this late afternoon and this time didn't know anyone there. As he opened the door, he heard the jukebox playing

"Smokey Mountain Rain," and wished how in the heat he could feel some of that rain right now. It was September, but the last few days felt like August.

He sat alone and had time to observe. Nothing better to do. It wasn't the sort of place you'd bring a book. He tried to figure out which one had the truck with the *Body-Soul* sticker, but could only guess.

Mounted on the wall was a thirty-six inch screen. Playing was Country TV brought in by the satellite dish on top of the store. It was on mute so as not to interfere with Alabama's lines. The scene on the TV was of two country boys racing a couple of identical black and white spotted milk cows. Riding bareback with no shoes. The boys were kicking the cows in the sides to get them to gallop along. Their full bags were flopping side to side. Chauncey reflected on Trig's saying how it was a lot easier to manage cows than people and you got an extra bonus in the fact that cows don't talk back. Chauncey smiled at the recollection. He remembered that Clint had said in one of his university classes in the agricultural school, the prof had asked how many tits a cow had, and one student had said two, and another eight, still another sixteen. Clint said he'd wondered what nuclear reactor these cows had been born near. The cows on the screen clearly displayed their right number.

One fellow in the restaurant was getting a real rise out of the cow-riding scene. He was laughing loud. The other people in the restaurant were trying not to laugh at him laughing. Chauncey heard a man at the next table say, "Don't take a whole lot to entertain Ronnie, I'll swear."

Somewhere in the Smokey Mountain rain... Randy Owen had wound up his song and now David Ball was taking his place. *Guess I got a thinking problem* he was singing.

Chauncey was glad it wasn't a Clemson football Saturday. The Grahams were fans, and the TV wouldn't have been on mute if the Tigers were playing. Chauncey glanced at a big orange tiger-paw flag flapping outside. Strange thing was the paw was a dog's paw-print, not a tiger's, but the football fans didn't care in the least. They were about as divorced from the reality of nature as the lad who'd thought a cow's bag had sixteen tits. Chauncey concluded that these were two more examples of the Nature Deficit Disorder that Clint had diagnosed.

Despite the flag and other signs of sports mania, Chauncey felt comfortable here. He liked the mounted big bass on the wall, the John Deere calendar that showed a different antique tractor for each month, the art prints picturing a local country store and old barns. In fact, the general feel of the place, minus TV, jukebox, and gadgets, reminded him a little of Kildee's Store. Yes, and there was a neon Miller sign, but even it had the blue neon head of a deer complete with heavy green neon rack that kind of made it alright, despite the weird colours. People talked and told stories in their booths and at their tables sort of like around Kildee's pot-bellied stove. Well, that was stretching it, but he tried to make the connection, doing everything he could every day, as his habit had become, to marry disparate and fragmented parts in today's atomized and departmentalised world—a world of divorces, he said. Pat had his place climate-controlled, a thing Kildee would never think of doing. Chauncey had to admit it was good to have a cool air-conditioned spot to go to today in this heat. The cold September nights preceding today had spoiled him.

Global warming, Chauncey thought. *All this weird weather, all these extremes. Weird's a word I use a lot these days. That and scam.*

He thought about the difference between Pat's and the majority of places in the urban world. For the most part, despite the commercial surface of brand names and brand games, this had the unmistakable stamp of *right here and nowhere else.*

Since the place sold beer, Chauncey, who didn't usually, had him one, a good brown bottle of Michelob Ultra that felt cold in his hand. He noticed most everybody else was drinking either Miller or Ice House. The barbecue was even better than the last time. Under his breath, Chauncey said "Damn." He couldn't believe his taste buds. He took a sip of beer and speared a fork of meat.

"Damn that's good," he said aloud this time. If only the beer was up to par with the barbecue. Pat's extra sweet tea was really what Chauncey felt went with the place, but today he was marking a special day.

Next time the waitress came by, he ordered another Michelob. Then he called her back. "Make it an Ice House this time," he said.

After his third beer, he watched the pretty young woman selecting a candy bar from the rack at the cash register. She was one of Pat's in-laws. She favoured Pat's wife a lot.

The waitress had high cheek bones and coal-black eyes. She had the look of the Cherokee. Some of the folks around the community had long ago intermarried with both Cherokee and Catawba tribes.

The world felt even better after the fourth beer. Every woman in the place had begun to look like a beauty queen. Even the overweight one who sat on the high lunch counter stool had poetic qualities. To Chauncey, perched up there on that slender support as she was, pale flesh overflowing all around, she looked like one of those fragile mushrooms that pop up on the lawn or in the woods after a rain. She was large, but large too had its charms.

The jukebox was silent now, and the TV was off mute and on Larry, the Cable Guy. The sound of his trademark "Git'er done" floated over the scene. Chauncey had just seen a wrecker in Clay Bank the other day with a decal on its back window saying **GIT'ER DONE.** Like Chauncey, the wrecker owner had named his vehicle with a female name. On its side in big red letters were the words **MISS BEHAVE**.

"Better than Blue Bessie," thought Chauncey. But he'd lived with the name so long, he wasn't about to change it now.

Today was Chauncey's sixtieth birthday. Some might be depressed at that, but he was happy. At one point in his life, he'd never thought he'd make it this far. Still, he wanted to celebrate alone, probably, he thought, the legacy of being an only child.

Lula Bess and Kildee had invited him over for supper. Dana had wanted to throw him a birthday party for their friends—cake, streamers, silly hats, and all. Chauncey had joked that so many candles on the cake would raise the heat index ten points, and it was already hot. Ida and Clint wanted to have Trig and Dana and him spend the evening with them. To all this, he'd given his sincere thanks and declined. Sometimes you just needed to be alone. That's what he was mostly use to anyway.

He was spending his birthday with the black bear Pat had mounted on the restaurant wall. Just right now, he liked having a companion he didn't have to make conversation with.

The bear was configured in such a way that it looked like he was coming into the restaurant through the wall. Only the front half of his body showed. His mouth was open and the sharp white teeth contrasted startlingly with the black fur. He had his right paw stretched before him like he was about to swat something or someone. He wasn't real happy. His claws were extended and were sharp and white as his teeth. Maybe he'd broken through the wall to get back at all these people who'd invaded and paved his woods. Couldn't blame him for being riled. Or maybe he was just trying to escape the Floridiots who'd built A-frame million dollar chalets on the Carolina mountainsides that he had used to call home. A bear could take seeing only so many jet-skiers on the artificial lakes that were once his favourite trout streams, special waterfalls, and huckleberry thickets.

A group of newcomers who'd got interested in the bear went out the side door. They were dressed like they might be from Columbia. The man had on a garnet and black Carolina Gamecock golf shirt. His little boy had on a matching one and a USC ball cap reading **Back to Back National Baseball Champs**. They were looking to see if the rear half of the bear was on the outside. The bear looked just that real.

So the bear was Chauncey's birthday companion, and with the fifth beer had begun to move. The bear's eyes followed him.

Chauncey had a glazed happy look on his face. He usually didn't drink over two beers and wasn't use to five. He was feeling them a lot in the heat. He knew this would have to be his last. He'd make the most of it.

He liked not having to think. This morning, after chores, it had been otherwise. He'd been studying his Virgil. *Sunt lachrymae rerum* he'd read. Virgil had it right. There *were* tears in the very nature of things. Sad to know you would leave friends and loved ones. Sad to lose the clear eyes that saw so much beauty in the familiar forests and fields. Sad to think of this landscape itself dissolving.

He knew death was a part of life, but that didn't make the passing of things less grievous. He couldn't help but feel an emptiness with the loss of someone or something of beauty. He just hoped that in his life he'd not been guilty of hastening the death of too many beautiful things, because he'd come to understand that it's only through beauty that death and loss are overcome. He'd come to the conclusion that progress isn't progress if it destroys anything beautiful.

Sunt lachrymae rerum he'd said aloud several times before it came to him that these sounds were strangely the closest human utterance to the red-tail hawk's sweetly plaintive cries that best caught the spirit of his place. He'd always thought that if he could one day put the hawk's cry into his own words, maybe capture it in the amber of his verse, then he could die satisfied. Now he found it had already been done for him. He wasn't disappointed at that. He didn't feel cheated, just relieved. It wasn't up to him now to do it after all.

Sixty years. Well, he was just proud he'd come through that long a time. Not that many of those years hadn't been a struggle just to carry on. If Dana had made him the cake she wanted to, he'd have insisted on sixty candles, one for every damn year. There was accomplishment in just existing over that length of time.

The juke box was playing a song Clint had introduced him to from his days at vet school. Clint said it was one of the few things he'd gotten from his sojourn there. Randall Bramblett was singing that in a dream he'd been riding along a country road and seen Christ twisted up in a barb-wire fence.

Pure Flannery O'Connor and from close to the same world, Chauncey thought. The singer was a rural South Georgia boy, with images of yellow rivers, curling vines coming through windows, porch lights, dusty cane fields, green moths on screens, pulpwood trucks, and bowing pines. The words came in a blur. *Jesup, Jesup Georgia,* Clint had said. That's the place. The refrain kept hitting him with the force of prize-fighter punches. About understanding it all one day. Even through the beer haze the notes had power to move him to the edge of his seat. The tune died away and another Bramblett song hushed the place for a time...his *angels appearing, waving welcome signs, but he seeing only come back some other time...standing there with his concrete mind.* Another of Clint's favourites.

Pat came over and sat down with him underneath the bear. He had an Ice House and was eating boiled peanuts, taking a little break from the hot kitchen.

"Glad to see you Chauncey. You're looking good."

"Feeling good too," Chauncey smiled. "Your barbecue is still the best I ever had."

"Thank you. Me and the boys try."

After a time of asking how the kin were and how things got along on the various farms, Pat said, "Hear Dana's moved back from Charlotte and her husband got in a wreck and killed hisself."

"That's right."

"Well you know my brother Killian dated Dana back in high school."

"Yeah. I remember that. He was real serious about her, well as I remember."

Pat paused, "Killian thought a lot of her. Hated when she moved. Said the other day that if he hadn't found Helen, he might have had a hard time forgetting."

"What did Helen say?"

"Just smiled and looked at the pictures of her five young'uns and the twelve grand-babies lined up on the wall. Guess that speaks louder than words."

"How's Killian anyway?"

"Fine. Told me he was glad Dana'd come back and y'all got engaged."

"Yep. I'm a happy man."

"She's a sweet woman. Been through a couple of rough patches. Deserves a break, Killian says."

They both paused. Chauncey took a sip of beer. He looked down at his plate. He piled the crumpled paper napkins on it and arranged his fork and spoon.

"But Pat, there's just one thing I got to know," he said. Chauncey looked serious.

There was a longer pause.

"It's really been bugging me," he said. Pause again.

Pat looked up at him. Pat and Killian were Dana's distant kin, and the families had been thick for a century at least. So Pat was expecting some personal thing by way of inquiry. Probably about Dana and maybe Dana and Killian.

Chauncey lifted his beer again. He looked at his plate and then back up at Pat.

"Just one thing, and I gotta soon go." Chauncey framed his question slowly. "Pat, what's the story on that bear?"

Pat was expecting a different sort of question, so after adjusting to the new path, he began his tale.

"Bear kept gettin' in my dumpster around back, shaking it, lifting up its lid. He wouldn't be shooed away, so I shot him with my sawed off shotgun."

Chauncey looked squarely at him. Five beers couldn't convince him of that and they made him brave enough to intimate Pat was playing light with the truth. And he was fully aware men didn't do that.

"Pat, there ain't no black bears that size around here," he said.

"You calling me a liar," Pat said.

"Don't like to use that word, but reckon I am."

"And to my face in my own restaurant?"

"Reckon so."

After a serious pause Pat's squinted grey eyes turned suddenly merry, and he laughed. "Yeah. Killian shot it up in Canada on one of his hunting trips. But I like to tell the tale. Makes a good story. Makes people think twice before they go in the woods. Makes the world more interesting. Wouldn't believe how many'd fall for it."

"And that's half the fun for you, ain't it?" Chauncey half asked, half commented.

"Yep. And a couple months ago two DNR agents and a Federal game warden came to call. Some self-appointed policeman reported me. 'You know, you just can't go around shooting bears,' they said, 'Even if they ain't supposed to be around here no more.' Killian happened to be here with me delivering a load of wood and after we played with the fellows awhile, and them beginning to mention fines, and maybe a jail sentence, Killian just laughed and gave them the taxidermist's receipt that he had handy in the cash drawer. A man up in Manitoba."

Chauncey laughed again, then shook his head slowly in commiseration.

"Well you know, Pat, even if you'd killed that bear, and I like bears a whole lot, I'd not turn you in. Some people got a damn lot to do."

Pat paused. "Chauncey, today there's some folks like to play at police. I reckon they love bear more than they love Pat."

Pat didn't look exactly hurt or angry, but he did look sad. "You got to have a permit for everything, and if you don't, you're breaking some law you probably never heard of."

Chauncey finished the last sip of his beer and so did Pat. Pat mounded up his boiled peanut shells in a neat pile and raked them into an empty dish, then went back to his register to let a customer pay his bill.

The jukebox was playing again. The TV was on mute during the news. This time it was Ray Price and Kitty Wells. Chauncey's head was spinning a little in a not unpleasant way and the music came blurred. *Heartaches and heartbreak,* the musicians sang, *troubles by the score.* They sang with a jaunty undefeated sound in their voices as they delivered the sad lines. *Understanding it all one day.*

Chauncey sat there awhile longer taking the sounds and sights of the restaurant in. The smells of food mingled into one. He watched two little boys throw darts at the board on the back wall. They weren't very good and kept missing the board. They ran to retrieve their errant arrows, horsing around as boys will.

Chad's little four-year-old was one of the boys. He already looked a lot like Pat.

Chauncey was letting the alcohol wear down. The rich barbecue was helping in that way. He took his time. There was no reason to rush home. He knew the sun would hit him full force when he walked out the door, so he was waiting for its rays to weaken some.

Twice he went to the restroom, and felt how good it was not to see graffiti scribbled on the wall over the commode. After another half hour and having just about enough of "Git'er Done," who was back on the TV, he left a tip and paid his bill. His head was clear.

Pat's wife Doris was at the register now. "Good to hear about you and Dana," she said. "I talked to her at the beauty parlor last week. She's so happy. Y'all please come over here any time."

"We sure will," Chauncey replied. "Dana's a great cook, but it will be good to give her a break now and then."

Doris smiled.

On his drive back through the white fields, he had the truck windows rolled down and his left arm outside. Soon these same acres would be brown with the prickly burrs of picked cotton bolls as far as the eye could see, up to the ragged line of dark woods, woods deep enough you could at least imagine bears the size of the one on Pat's wall. The tastes and the smells of the restaurant lingered in his consciousness even as the fresh fragrant air of the countryside blew through the cab. Every now and then, there was a cool breeze like a breath from the deep woods.

Terroir, he said aloud to the familiar landscape, understanding the French appellation for all that came together to give a place its own particular taste distinct from all others on earth, like he knew the taste of his own well water sure and distinct.

Yes, he'd gotten so he could taste place. His palate had become refined to it. Repeating *terroir* and liking the sound of it against the truck's clatter, he refused to credit the brown patches and mutilated trees on road's edge. As he drove on, he began to hum Singin' Billy Walker's old hymn tunes, "Sweet Prospect," "Thorny Desert," and then his favorite, "French Broad"—*High o'er the hills the mountains rise, their summits tower toward the skies; then will I sing God's praises there, who brought me through my troubles here.* He circled back to his favorite lines, *Sweet fields arrayed in living green and rivers of delight.* The songs soothed and satisfied him in some way that Alabama and Kitty Wells just couldn't do.

The songs led him to think of Trig. He broke off his tune and chuckled. He was remembering a comment his friend had made at the store a few days ago. A customer had been baiting him about why he didn't get an indoor bathroom. "Get up with the times," he'd said. And Trig was quick as ever with his answer that he didn't reckon there was anything wrong with an indoor commode as long as you didn't have to kneel down and worship it.

Chauncey knew exactly what Trig meant. How could "Standard of Living" be measured, as it was by the agencies, by the number of TV's, telephones, and commodes you had. There was a whole way of seeing in Trig's words. It was more than a solemn condemnation of the consumer society. Chauncey knew exactly what Trig meant. This having comfort at all cost had led to an idolatry that robbed people of joy. Modern efficiency had tried to make man more than he was, and in doing so, he'd become a lot less. To Chauncey, the true *more* reverberated in all Singin' Billy's songs, in what he was, and in what he bequeathed. Of this progressive standard of living, he felt that those in his community had more than a standard of living. They had a standard of faith.

"Old Trig." He'd have to remember to pass his friend's reply about the commode on to Dana tomorrow morning. She'd sure get a kick out of it too.

CLAY BANK COUNTY
HENDERSONS ISLAND
SHELTON FERRY ROAD
OLD CALEBS FARM
UNCLE GILLIAMS RIVER SHANTY
SEEKWELL A.M.E. CHURCH
WHERE THE BUFFALO HERD BLOCKED THE ROAD
OXNER FAMILY CEMETERY
LYLES FAMILY CEMETERY
OLD FERRY ROAD
RICHARDS CEMETERY
BROAD RIVER
WEEPING MARY CHURCH
OLD CEMETERY

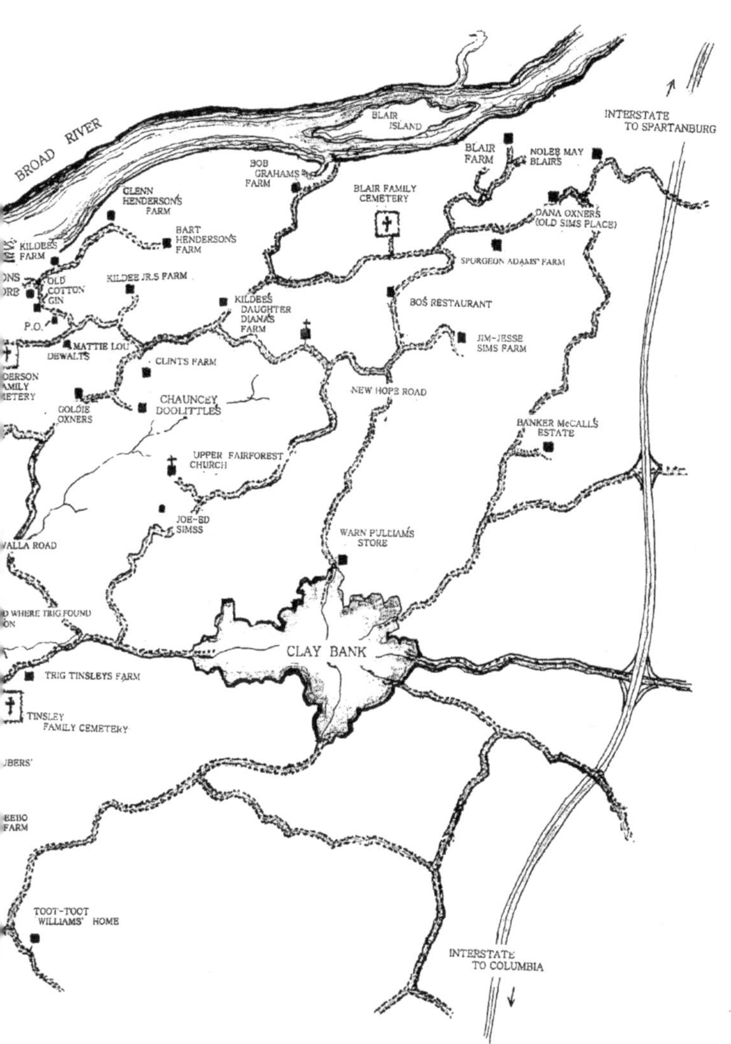
BROAD RIVER
BLAIR ISLAND
INTERSTATE TO SPARTANBURG
BLAIR FARM
NOLEB MAY BLAIRS
BOB GRAHAMS FARM
GLENN HENDERSON'S FARM
BLAIR FAMILY CEMETERY
DANA OXNERS (OLD SIMS PLACE)
BART HENDERSON'S FARM
KILDEES FARM
SPURGEON ADAMS' FARM
KILDEE JR.S FARM
OLD COTTON GIN
BOS RESTAURANT
KILDEES DAUGHTER DIANAS FARM
P.O.
JIM-JESSE SIMS FARM
MATTIE LOU DEWALTS
CLINTS FARM
NEW HOPE ROAD
CHAUNCEY DOOLITTLES
GOLDIE OXNERS
BANKER McCALLS ESTATE
UPPER FAIRFOREST CHURCH
JOE-ED SIMSS
WARN PULLIAMS STORE
CLAY BANK
TRIG TINSLEYS FARM
TINSLEY FAMILY CEMETERY
TOOT-TOOT WILLIAMS' HOME
INTERSTATE TO COLUMBIA

About the Author

JAMES KIBLER was born in Prosperity, South Carolina, and graduated from the University of South Carolina with a Ph.D. in English. His interests have lead him to write on diverse subjects, from botany and agriculture to architecture and art. As literary man, he has written in several genres, including the novel, short story, and poetry. The history and saga of the renovation of his plantation house is chronicled in his critically acclaimed *Our Fathers' Fields*, which was awarded the prestigious Fellowship of Southern Writers Award for Nonfiction.

It is rare for a writer to excel as both a creative artist and a scholar, but James Kibler has achieved such distinction. For many years Professor of English at the University of Georgia, he has written authoritatively on many aspects of Southern literature. As scholar, Kibler is largely responsible for the contemporary rise of William Gilmore Simms studies. He is the founding editor of *Simms Review*, author of the definitive work on Simms's poetry, and the discoverer of many previously unknown Simms writings.

Dr. Kibler is currently completing his fifth novel, *The Gentler Gamester*.

Green Altar Books

SHOTWELL PUBLISHING

Columbia, S.C.

www.ingramcontent.com/pod-product-compliance
Lightning Source LLC
Chambersburg PA
CBHW060548310726
48982CB00008B/1049/J

* 9 7 8 0 9 9 7 9 3 9 3 2 3 *